MAC SLATER HUNTS THE COOL

Mac Slater

HUNTS THE COOL

TRISTAN BANCKS

SIMON & SCHUSTER BOOKS FOR YOUNG READERS

NEW YORK   LONDON   TORONTO   SYDNEY

SIMON & SCHUSTER BOOKS FOR YOUNG READERS
An imprint of Simon & Schuster Children's Publishing Division
1230 Avenue of the Americas, New York, New York 10020

Originally published as *Mac Slater, Coolhunter: The Rules of Cool* in Australia in 2008 by Random House Australia Pty Ltd
Published by arrangement with Random House Australia Pty Ltd
First U.S. edition April 2010

For information about special discounts for bulk purchases, please contact Simon & Schuster Special Sales at 1-866-506-1949 or business@simonandschuster.com.
The Simon & Schuster Speakers Bureau can bring authors to your live event. For more information or to book an event, contact the Simon & Schuster Speakers Bureau at 1-866-248-3049 or visit our website at www.simonspeakers.com.
Book design by Chloë Foglia
The text for this book is set in Bembo.
Manufactured in the United States of America
0310 FFG
10 9 8 7 6 5 4 3 2 1

Library of Congress Cataloging-in-Publication Data
Bancks, Tristan.
Mac Slater hunts the cool / Tristan Bancks.—1st ed.
p. cm.
Summary: Mac, an Australian youth, has one week to prove that he can be a "coolhunter," identifying emerging trends and posting images on a website, but he is competing against a classmate on whom he has a crush and dealing with resistance from his best friend and his own confusion over what "cool" means.
ISBN 978-1-4169-8574-7
[1. Popular culture—Fiction. 2. Video recording—Fiction. 3. Blogs—Fiction. 4. Beaches—Fiction. 5. Schools—Fiction. 6. Australia—Fiction.] I. Title.
PZ7.B21766Mac 2010
[Fic]—dc22
2009000152

Dedicated to
Huxley, Luca, and Amber Melody. Dreamers, all.

Thanks to
Graham Sutherland and Eddie Gray for their advice.

Author Note

The characters and events in this story are fictional. Please don't take their actions as tips on how to fly. If you want to learn to fly, get in touch with the U.S. Hang Gliding and Paragliding Association (www.ushpa.aero) and find out where you can learn from the pros. Don't teach yourself. No really. Don't.

Oh, and the characters in this book also pull off some crazy stunts. Don't try them at home. I can't write you out of danger like I can with these guys.

Coolhunters

Coolhunters are teens and twenty-somethings with their fingers on the pulse of the freshest, hottest ideas and innovations coming off the street. The people who recognize cool stuff way before anyone else sees it. Big companies rely on coolhunters to tell them what's up and to give feedback on shoes, clothes, and technology before they hit shelves. Coolhunters influence what we eat, wear, listen to, drive, ride, watch, and buy.

Born to Fly

It was our greatest invention ever: a flying bike. Paul and I had been obsessed with building a flying machine for years. The thing I loved and hated about being that guy's best friend was that whenever we dreamed up something like this, I was always the guinea pig.

"I'm the brains of us, Mac," he'd always tell me. "You're the guts." Which was his way of saying that he knew the thing was going to crash.

So, there I was at the top of Kings Cliff Hill. Helmet on, clutching the grips on a lowrider bike with homemade solar engine. Wind was blowing in over the rock face from the ocean, blasting us. Clouds, the enemy of solar power, were gathered all around. The footpath followed the line of the cliff, soaring downhill to the park in front of the beach where the jump was.

The bike was made totally from stuff we'd found at the dump. Seven bikes, a washing machine, two Weedwackers, and a fold-out bed had given their lives to the development of this baby. Paul designed it and we built it together. A whole year, it took, mainly because of the motor. I just hoped it wasn't going to be another shocker like our Backpack Solo Helicopter with ceiling-fan blades. My leg had only just healed.

Paul hit record on the skanky old video camera we'd taped to the front of the bike.

"Flick it," he said.

I flipped the switch and the solar engine gasped into life. Paul did final checks on the hundred or so strings that led from the bike to the paragliding wing behind me. The wing was shaped like a narrow parachute, but while a parachute was made for dropping from the sky, a wing was made for soaring through it. We'd borrowed it from my dad's shed. He was "away" for a little while. But we'll get to that.

The deal was that I'd charge downhill to the park, top speed, the wing would fill with air, rise above me, I'd hit the wooden jump—specially built for the event—launch into the air, and fly. No one had ever done it. Not round here, anyway.

Paul clicked my helmet clasp and adjusted his thick black glasses. His hair was wild, like he'd just climbed out of bed. He wore a tight white T-shirt with a pic of Brin and Page, the Google guys, on the front. The sleeves hugged his skinny arms. His teeth looked like a fence that had been hit by a car.

"Remember, man. This is gonna make you so rock-'n'-roll. We fly and we're gonna be made men in this town." Paul thought all our inventions would make us "made men" in Kings Bay.

I looked down the hill to where about fifty people had gathered. I'd been promoting this thing all week. I kinda figured, rather than die quietly, I might as well get it filmed on a bunch of kids' phones. I knew the chance of me dying was the only reason anyone had showed. I think we'd even used it in our text campaign.

Ten or eleven kids were lying down on the other side of the jump ramp. I'd given them a personal guarantee I wouldn't use their heads as a landing strip. Even a bike that couldn't fly could clear ten kids. Nine, at least. And our test run had gone pretty good. It was only down Paul's driveway, which was about fifty times shorter and less steep than Kings Cliff Hill, but we'd gotten air. I'd flown for a few seconds and done a supersweet landing in the cul-de-sac.

Then I'd kept going down his neighbor's drive and smashed into the back of their Camry. But that was just bad luck.

"Give me your phone," I said to Paul.

He gave it. I switched to camera, zoomed in, and scanned around to find Cat DeVrees standing near the jump. She was in our year's *A* group—angry, cold-blooded, and totally hot. She had hair that changed every time you saw her (today, jet black, dead straight, square bangs) and a lip ring, and she pretty much owned our grade. She probably didn't even know I was in our grade, but she would in about three minutes' time. She was hanging with two older guys. They looked like they were from the city. Their clothes stuck out in our beach town—way too formal. I could see them all laugh, and then Cat looked right at me and stuck her finger up. Adrenaline shot into my gut and I gave the phone back to Paul.

I looked down at my clothes. Gray shorts and socks. Green polo. School uniform is so not a good look on a Sunday afternoon, but they were the only semiclean clothes I had. See, my mom twirls fire for a living and she's not that big on domestic stuff.

"I don't think I want to do this," I said to Paul. "I'm not a great rider. Riding down here even without flying freaks me."

"Don't be a loser. You love it," he said.

He knew me too well.

"I guess," I said. "You really think it's all right with these clouds?"

"Yeah," Paul said, looking out over the cliff face, biting his lip. "Should be."

A cloud passed overhead and the engine coughed, then kicked in again.

"Well, how about you do it, then?" I suggested.

Paul gave me a look. "Not funny."

Paul was deeply afraid of flying. One of his many fears.

"Okay, give me time to get down and into position. I'll give you the sign," he said.

Paul bolted off. "Be scary!" he screamed over the sound of

the engine as he legged it down the steepest slope in Kings.

A couple of minutes later he gave me the thumbs-up. I fed the engine some throttle and took off. Dragging the wing behind was super–slow going, like riding through maple syrup. I started to wonder if the engine was strong enough to get the wing up when, suddenly, it began to lift. I looked back just in time to see the wind slap it to the ground again.

By halfway down I must have been doing forty miles an hour. The footpath smeared past and, down below, I could see kids cheering but all I could hear was the wind hissing in my ears, urging me not to do this. Just as I hit the steepest part of the hill, the wing shot up into the air like a rocket and nearly snatched me up and over the cliff face.

I worked hard and somehow grounded the bike again. A thick bank of clouds swept overhead and the solar engine choked and died just as I hit the flat at the bottom of the hill. I was going to need engine power to keep my speed up, but the cloud shadow darkened. I was twenty yards from the jump, heading toward the beach but losing speed. So I pedaled harder.

With twenty yards to go, a bunch of kids lying under the jump chickened and rolled out of the way. I thought about bailing too, but then I caught a glimpse of Cat DeVrees, mouth open, goggling me. The crowd was packed tight, leaving a nar-row path to the jump. No space to ditch.

I heard my front tire hit the bottom of the ramp and I

started wishing that thing up into the air. A blast of wind blew the wing hard to the left and back again to the right. Just as I hit the lip, another few kids rolled out from in front of the jump.

Two hardcore dudes were still lying there, four yards in front of the ramp. One of them was a guy they called Egg—a massive sophomore football player. Cat's boyfriend. No wonder she was there. I closed my eyes, praying I'd clear him. The bike left the jump and I felt it pull upward. The bike weighed nothing. I was flying. Actually flying. Way higher than on the test. I opened my eyes and saw beach and ocean in front of me. I felt like I was gonna fly right out over the fence and onto the sand. It was gold.

Then a gust of wind blew out of nowhere and tore the wing sideways. I'd seen kite surfers get smashed when this happened to them. And water's softer than earth. The wind was ripping me out of the air. The crowd cleared. A few kids fell in the rush.

The wing hit ground and BAM! I hit right after.

My head, shoulder, and rib cage slammed into gravel, dirt, and grass. The bike clipped somebody's ankle. Kids ran screaming from the wreckage. It was like one of those air-show disasters they have at the end of the news. Only I'd just seen it from the cockpit.

Everything went quiet.

⊲ Speed and Tony ⊳

Kkkkkkkkkkkkkk. The mangled bike wheel scraped over concrete as we dragged ourselves along the edge of the road out of town. My head was bandaged, my ankle twisted, my whole body scraped bloody. Paul had the torn parachute under his arm. The video camera was shredded. Only the handle remained. The bike was a write-off but Paul just couldn't let go.

I'd been trying to cheer him up. He hadn't said a word since the crash—not that he was worried about my injuries. He was just devastated to see a year of his life totaled in front of a crowd.

Most kids had disappeared as soon as the disaster went down. I guess the few that stayed must've dragged me into the surf club. Then a fat man with lumps on his face gave me first aid and suggested that my brains were made of crap for attempting such an insane stunt.

It started to rain. It felt good on my scrapes. I stopped and raised my face to the sky. Then I started laughing for no reason, which is the worst kind, 'cause you can't stop laughing if you don't know what you're laughing about. Paul stopped a few yards on.

"What?" he said.

"I dunno. Just . . . funny," I said, looking at the sky.

Paul looked at me. "Dipstick," he said.

"What? We gave it a shot," I said. "We crashed and burned. Onward and upward, duders."

"No. You crashed and burned," he said.

"Yeah," I said. "But, before that, I was actually flying. I must've been up there for, like, two minutes."

"Seconds," said Paul.

"Whatever. It felt like a long time," I said. "Anyway, what happened to the solar engine? You're the brains of us, remember? I'm just the loser who's prepared to die for the cause."

"I didn't know a couple of clouds would kill it," he said.

"Yeah, well, next time, let's not use the solar panels off your calculator to power a bike," I said, starting to laugh again.

"They weren't off m—"

We turned to the sound of tires on gravel close behind us. A black Jeep Commander—big and square, Hummer-style, with dark tinted windows—pulled up next to us. The front passenger window slid down. Inside was one of the dudes who had been with Cat DeVrees. He was maybe thirty-something, black spiky hair, chiseled jaw.

"Need a ride?" he said in an English accent.

"No, we're okay," I said.

"That was pretty cool out there," he said.

"Thanks," I replied. "Glad we entertained you."

"No, seriously. We'd like to talk to you. Jump in. Get out of the rain. Look, Cat's in here."

A rear window wheeled down to reveal Cat DeVrees inside, playing with her lip ring, blowing and popping little pink gum bubbles. She faked a smile. I looked to Paul to see if we should get in. He frowned as if to say, "No way."

"What's your name?" I said to the guy.

"Speed," he said. "This is Tony."

Tony was behind the wheel—a big, kind of European-looking dude with slicked-back hair, about forty I guessed. He flicked the wipers on.

"Hi," I said. "Look, we don't know you and all that, so . . ."

"But, Mac, we know you. You live in a bus with your mom over in the Arts Village, right?"

"How do you know that?" I asked.

"Let's talk somewhere else," he said. "Name your place."

"Sobu," said Cat from inside. Sobu was a Japanese restaurant where rich people in Kings Bay hung out, i.e., not me and Paul.

Paul whispered in my ear: "How about the Bardo?"

I nodded and said, "My mom's got a stall down in the Bardo Market. Let's meet there."

"Do you know where that is?" Speed asked Cat.

She nodded reluctantly and snapped another bubble.

"See you there in fifteen," said Speed. "You'll want to hear what we have to say."

The windows closed and the Commander spun around, spat gravel, and turned back into town.

Paul's eyes had come alive.

"You reckon they want the rights to the bike?" he asked.

I looked at the carcass of the bike lying on the ground.

"Somehow I don't think so," I said.

The Bardo Market

We entered the market from the back alley. We were soaked. Paul clutched the remains of our "flying" bike, which he'd now decided was about to make us wealthy beyond our wildest dreams. We wove our way through the maze of tiny mystical stalls filled with incense, Buddhas, and jewelry. Beads and baskets hung from the low ceiling. Years ago the market had been just a collection of stalls on Friday nights but now it was a permanent fixture. Bored stall-owners drank herbal tea and read thick books with titles like *Sudden Awakening*.

Mom was sitting at her stand—long dark hair, green eyes—making flaming batons. She'd started the biz after she and Dad separated. Hardly anyone bought the batons but she kept making them anyway. I told her people'd go nuts for them on the Web but she was the full anti-tech chick. We didn't even have a computer at home.

"Sweetheart!" she cried when she saw my wet blood-splattered bandage. "What happened to your head?"

"Wipeout," I said.

"Hmmm. Bike didn't fly?"

Paul looked guilty. Mom was the only one of our folks we'd told about the attempt. She was the only one who wouldn't freak. Paul's folks reckoned she was "permissive."

"Hello, Paul," she said, out of habit.

Paul looked down like he hadn't heard her. He was one of those kids who refused to speak to adults. In the eight years I'd known him, the only adults I'd seen him speak to were his parents, and only if it meant life or death. He reckoned he had gerontophobia—fear of old people. "They make me think of porridge dripping out of a toothless mouth onto an old, wrinkly chin," he'd say. Go figure.

"Let's get some papaya ointment on those cuts," Mom said.

She thought homemade papaya ointment was the answer to everything.

"Hey, Mac," said a voice. It was Speed, with Tony and Cat. "Cool market."

Cat was pulling the neck of her top up over her nose as if she couldn't stand the smell of the place. She lowered it briefly to sip a take-out coffee, probably through one of her dad's lids. Mr. DeVrees made a killing selling plastic lids. Totally unrecyclable. My mom had a stat that you could circle the earth a bunch of times with the number of take-out coffee lids humans toss out every year.

"I'm Speed Cohen," he said to my mom, shaking hands. "We have a little proposition for your son."

"Right," Mom said, supersuspicious.

"It's cool, Ma," I said. "Can we go out back?"

Eyeing Speed and big serious Tony, she parted the purple curtain behind her and let us into the small, warmly lit back room. The walls were covered with dark red material and there was a table in the middle where Mom sometimes did Tarot readings. Paul leaned the mashed bike frame against the wall, adjusting it to get the best angle.

"Wow," said Speed, looking around the room. "This is sweet."

He, Tony, Paul, and I took a seat. Cat sighed loudly.

"So . . ." I said.

"Guess you're wondering what all this is about," said Speed. He looked to Tony, who gave him a single nod.

"Well, we have a website you may have heard of called Coolhunters." He waited for my reaction but I'd never heard of it. Cat gave me a filthy look and pulled a *Vogue* mag out of her bag. She was so hot when she was angry. Which was always.

"Well, anyway, we have this network of coolhunters, right? And they . . . Do you know what a coolhunter is?" he asked, not waiting for a response. "It's someone who hunts cool."

"Yeah, I kinda figured," I said. Paul flicked me a glare, and Speed went on.

"Like, say a company's about to launch a new phone or game or shoe. They come to us and our coolhunters tell them whether kids are going to dig it or not."

"Right," I said.

Mom came in with a Chinese teapot and five little cups and then left again.

"We're getting over a million unique hits a day from teens who form a worldwide network of coolhunters. They tell us what's hot everywhere on the planet. But we want five featured hunters to be the face of our site. We've got a kid in New York, one cruising South America, one in Shanghai, and another in Paris. We need somebody at the beach, and Kings Bay is so hot right now, we want someone on the ground here."

See, Kings has the best climate and some of the greatest surf on earth as well as this alternative greeny history. It was put on the map by a couple of surfers, two brothers, who hit the pro tour at fifteen. Then a couple of movie stars bought houses here and, bud-a-bam, overnight we went from backwater hippie haven, population nine thousand, to coolest vacation place on the planet.

"We've been watching you for a couple of months, Mac. You and a dozen other kids from this place," said Speed. "We've been reading your blog. We think you're interesting."

"My blog's anonymous," I shot back.

"You can find out anything on the Web," said Speed.

I swallowed hard, knowing all the stuff I'd written in that

blog, stuff I'd never tell anyone. I scanned my mind, trying to think how they might have found out it was me. Hacked into my profile somehow? I'd registered my name and stuff, but no one could see that. Maybe they did a search on blogs with refs to Kings Bay or something. Whatever it was, it sounded Dodge City. Or maybe he was lying.

"What do you know about me?" I asked, calling his bluff.

"How's your dad?" said Speed. My stomach sank. "When's he get out?"

Cat looked up, and if I didn't know how tough I was, I'd say I nearly had tears in my eyes. Nobody knew about my dad, except Paul. Speed saw my reaction and pushed on.

"Now . . . I'm going to ask you some questions. Just answer as honestly as you can," he said. "How often do you go out?"

"Out?" I asked, still reeling from the dad stuff. "Like, out of the house?"

Cat laughed.

"No, like to parties or on dates with girls," said Speed.

"Well, I dunno, kind of never, I s'pose."

"Okay," said Speed. "How do you find out about the latest trends?"

"What do you mean?"

"Well," said Speed. "Do you read mags, surf the Web, talk to friends? How do you find out what's cool?"

"I don't know," I said. *I don't even know what cool is,* I thought to myself.

"Right," said Speed. Cat put her mag down so she could watch the carnage.

"Well, tell me about this school-uniform-on-the-weekend thing," Speed said.

I looked down at my blood-stained uniform. Cat's face spread into a smile.

"That's totally cool," said Speed. I looked up. Cat's smile dropped.

"Where'd you get that from? That's total anarchy, man. It's, like, the reverse of refusing to wear your uniform to school. Parents and teachers would hate you wearing uniform on the weekend, yeah? And you're doin' it."

"I just don't have that many clothes," I said. Tony laughed a big deep laugh. Speed gave me a weird handshake. I didn't know when to punch knuckles and when to slide skin.

"This guy is an Innovator," Tony said with a French accent, the first words he'd spoken.

"And, like the best, he doesn't even know it!" said Speed.

"At school he's, like, not even on the map. He's a freak," said Cat.

"At least he's not a stuck-up cow," Paul snapped.

"Chill," said Speed.

"What's an Innovator?" I asked.

"Someone who's going off-map," Speed said. "Doing their own thing. Someone who does stuff and other people follow, yeah?"

"He's so not an Innovator," said Cat. "As if anyone's going to start wearing a uniform on the weekend and trying to make their bike fly."

"I'll tell you what we're going to do," said French Tony, ignoring Cat. He had this energy that commanded everyone's attention. "We are going to give each of you a week to prove yourselves. Cat and Mac, we'll give you each a camera and you will vlog whatever you think is cool about Kings Bay every day for the next week. Our subscribers will decide who they want."

Cat looked like she wanted to scratch my eyes out.

"And then what happens?" I asked.

"The winner becomes one of our five coolhunters," Speed told me. "You'll be our surfer guy and cover Kings Bay and we'll send you phones, skateboards, new game consoles, loads of stuff to try before it hits shelves. You vlog it, say what you think. We'll pay you. If the subscribers like you, you stay. If not, you're gone. The Chosen Five are meeting in New York City in a month's time."

New York? I wondered if he'd read that in my blog too. I'm, like, obsessed with New York. If I could go to any place, it'd be New York. It's the opposite of my life. Subway trains, steam through gutters, rats in sewers, the Lower East Side, people from all over the world making movies and music, writing books, creating stuff, innovating, putting it all on the line. I love where I'm from but, to me, if you're gonna go anywhere, you go to

New York. Even to smell the place. That's just the way it is.

I could see my mom's shadow on the curtain. I knew what she'd think of all this. And I knew she was listening. I tried to act cool, like I didn't want it so much.

"Well, I don't know," I said. "Cat seems to want it pretty bad, and I don't know how fired up I am about being in some kinda popularity contest."

Paul kicked me under the table.

"Well, it's up to you, man," said Speed. "Like I said, we've been tracking a bunch of kids so we could get someone else to trial, or we could just give Cat the gig. She's cute and she's very right for it. But you're a wild card and I like wild cards."

Cat gave me the deadliest of death stares. Paul kicked me again, harder this time, and I realized why.

"Well, see, Paul and I are kind of a team," I said.

"This isn't a school project, Mac. It's you we're interested in. Not your friend. Your call. Are you in or are you out?"

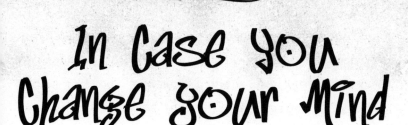

In Case You Change Your Mind

I crossed the rusty railway track that separated town from the Arts Village. The track hadn't seen a train in years, not since the airport was built twenty minutes away.

I entered the complex through the low timber reception area. The village was home to dozens of artists, healers, and backpackers. Rainbow headbands and hairy armpits were the uniform. It was one of the few places in town that hadn't been yuppified. The owners had been battling for years to fend off a company that wanted to level it, build sixteen stores and twenty-seven apartments, and make a bundle.

Just inside reception, a sunburned Danish backpacker was peeling skin off her boyfriend's back while they checked in. A bank of Web computers were all booked with a dozen travelers bashing away on keyboards in different languages.

I passed through reception and made a beeline toward our bus. My arms were killing me from lugging two heavy green shopping bags full of fruit and veggies all the way home. I passed a few twenty-something chicks carving wooden masks over near the beach track. Ken, a Hare Krishna dude with robes and a bald head, shuffled by eating a bowl of strange white goo. A dog snapped at flies. Smoke curled out of one of the tepees next to our bus.

Jewels Piper, a chick I'd grown up with, was sitting on the edge of the ti-tree lake, drawing designs on her shoes, a magazine lying on the ground beside her. Jewels was born in a tent at the village and lived in it for the first two years of her life. Then her mom left town and her dad, a poet, upgraded to a giant tepee. I don't know if you've heard but there's not a lot of big money in poetry these days, so Jewels dresses kind of crunchy, like me. She's a total original, but like any kid from a weird upbringing, all she really wants is to be normal. Meanwhile, all the normal kids are trying to be weird. Paul reckons she has a crush on me but I think Paul has one on her.

"Hey, Mac," she called out.

"Hey," I said, not stopping.

"Wanna hang out?"

"Nah," I said. I wasn't in the mood.

Jewels looked a bit hurt and went back to doodling on her shoe.

I rounded the corner of our bus—double-decker, painted decades back with lots of little murals and quotes like "Think

Global, Act Local," "Be You!," and the one my mom loves: "Vegetarians save the world! It takes 100,000 quarts of water to raise 2 pounds of beef!" The bus had wheels that hadn't turned in about two million years. Mom and Dad had driven it round the country before it died on this spot. They took it as a sign and stayed. I was born a year later, then my folks separated when I was about three. Now Mom and I live in a bus but we don't have a car. Work that out.

The bus faced the ramshackle wooden fence that separated the village from the new chicken factory next door. They "processed" 18,000 chickens a day in there and, when the wind was against us, the stench was deadly.

"Mac," said a voice. I turned. It was Mr. Kim, the old Korean dude with dreads who owned the complex. He was smiling as usual, carrying a big package wrapped in brown paper. "This came for you. Ten minutes ago," he said.

I plunked down the shopping bags and he handed it over. *"Annyeonghi kyeseyo,"* he said, and left. He was always trying to school us in Korean.

The package had an envelope taped to the front. On it were these words:

Mac

In case you change your mind.

-Speed

Mom arrived next to me with a couple more bags.

"What's that?" she said.

I just looked at her, turned, and shoved open the rear fold-in doors of the bus. I wasn't up for a discussion on morals or ethics or whatever.

The Driver's Seat

Mac

In case you change your mind.

-Speed

I read it for the tenth time. "In case you change your mind." And I knew I could. All I had to do was rip open the wrapping. I was desperate to see what was inside. I had a strong hunch what the big box was but I wasn't too sure about the little one strapped to the side. Maybe I could just look inside the envelope. But if I opened it, I knew I'd want to do the trial even more. I held it up to the fading sun to see if I could read anything through the wrapping. I was sitting in the driver's seat of our bus. I always sat there and thought about stuff. A bunch of old gauges without needles, a rusty spring poking through the seat into my butt, wipers that had stopped halfway through a wipe, now piled with leaves and dirt. Through the windshield I could see workers wearing white, milling around in the fluoro-lit chicken factory.

I decided to rip a little corner of the packaging. But then I thought about what Paul had said at the back of the Bardo Market after we'd left: "We're Mac and Paul, man. Like Mac and cheese. Dogs and fleas. We go together. Do you really want to do this by yourself?"

"Are you kidding? New York!" I'd said. "We can take our inventions, sell our ideas, skate in the sewers, live the dream, man! This is our shot."

"Your shot. Do whatever you think's right," he'd said, turning away, sulking. He always got weird when I was asked to do stuff without him.

I knew my mom would hate the whole coolhunting thing too. On the way home, she said: "Well, I think you did the right thing by saying no. You're not a consumerist kid, Mac. That's not us. And it sounds like you'd be encouraging more people to fly to Kings, clocking up carbon miles, and helping big companies to sell kids more things that they don't need."

She was probably right, I s'pose. And I couldn't do it without Paul. But they were talking New York and I'd dreamed of going there forever and it all sounded really cool, y'know? And listen to this:

Mac Slater, coolhunter.

Got a ring to it, huh?

The sun disappeared behind the chicken factory and the sea breeze blew a bunch of stink in through the open window. I reached for the old-school knob you used to wind the window up and it snapped off in my hand. Typical. I tossed it onto the floor and climbed out of the driver's seat and up the stairs to my room. I threw the box onto my bed and stopped for a second to look at the map of New York City stuck to my window. (There's not a lot of wall space when you live in a bus.) Lexington Avenue. Canal Street. Rockefeller Center. Tribeca. Little Italy. Harlem. Brooklyn. All these places I'd dreamed of going and now I had the chance. I took the stairs three at a time and sneaked out the back door of the bus, taking a right toward reception.

I clicked "Michiko" and a profile of a kooky Japanese photographer/skater chick from the 'burbs of Paris came up. She was one of the "Chosen Five" on the Coolhunters site.

I was in the Backpacker Café in the Arts Village. A girl with B. O. was pounding away on Facebook next to me, mumbling stuff under her breath in German.

Michiko's "likes" were listed as plastic cheese, Apple, handbags, hot sauce, Green Day, camouflage underwear, and graffiti art. Her dislikes were: London, tourists, baseball, geeks, oatmeal, and Picasso paintings. There was a whole bunch of other stuff too, telling us her take on the world. People got to vote on whether they thought she was cool or clueless. Her gauge was firmly in the cool.

There were more than a million profiles, including Michiko's and the other three coolhunters who'd been selected. The three other "chosen ones" were Van (a self-confessed NYC rich girl and tech expert), Luca (a South American adventure-sport guy), and Rash (a music- and movie-obsessed dude from Shanghai, China, who hates going outside).

Pretty different, but they all seemed to know what was cool. I wondered what my profile would look like if it was up there, but I had no idea about cool. At least I didn't think I did. Still, something inside me wanted to be one of them and I needed to open that package more than anything.

I quickly logged on to my blog. I had quite a few regular readers. (I wondered how many other people, like Speed, knew that I was me—if you know what I mean.) People often commented on the stuff I wrote, so I thought I'd put the question to them:

what do you do if your best friend is trying to hold you back from something you really want to do, just because they can't be involved? do u play for the team and just miss out or do you go ahead and do it anyway and look like a self-centered

pig who'll ditch their friends for the right opportunity? i'm talking about something that would really be cool for you and might involve say a trip to new york (or something) but this other dude won't let you do it without them?

I re-read what I'd written, selected it all, hit delete, then googled "New York City."

⟻ Monday ⟼

Someone dropped their shoulder into me. Another kid palmed me in the face. I shoved back, trying to hold my ground.

Getting on the bus was hell. Every morning the same thing. Fifteen kids in a flying wedge all trying to get through a doorway two feet wide at the same time. I needed to start skating to school again.

I shouldered my way up and on and was rammed down into the belly of the bus where kids were packed so tight that every time you turned a corner you ended up sitting on some weird dude's lap or with your head buried in a hot girl's armpit.

I landed a couple of yards away from Paul. Through the crowd he raised his eyebrow at me, then kept looking out the window. Still annoyed.

I dipped low and burrowed through the mosh pit, poking my head back up when I was next to him.

"Hey!" I said over the roar of bus and kids.

"Hey," he said.

"Guess what?" I said, smiling, trying to soften him up.

"What?" He frowned, knowing I was being weird and creepy.

"I looked on the Web last night," I said.

"Awesome," he said.

"There's this massive Imaginator Invention Fest in New York in a few weeks."

He tried to pretend this didn't interest him.

"Yeah," he said.

"It might be when this coolhunter meeting thing happens there. If we get the bike in the sky again, maybe I can take it there, sell our idea, license it to someone, y'know. It might be, like, a first step toward us being proper inventors and stuff."

He snorted. "That's a lot of maybes."

"Yeah, well, here's a couple more: Maybe you can come," I said. "Maybe we can save the bucks somehow."

I knew this was stretching it a bit. And we both knew that Paul would probably be too scared to get on the plane.

"Whatever, man. Like I said, if you want to do it, just do it." But he said it in that way that parents say stuff, so you know that you'd better not do it or they'll kill you.

"Why are you being such a baby about this?" I said. "We've always wanted to go to New York. Some random dude comes up and offers us the chance—"

"Offers *you* the chance," he corrected.

"Offers me the chance and you become this total loser and tell me not to do it."

"Well, do it then," he said. "No one's stopping you, coolhunter boy."

He said "coolhunter" like it was a dirty word.

"I will then," I snapped back.

"Good."

"Good."

And that was that.

The A Group

Don't look, don't look, don't look, don't look, don't look, I said over and over in my mind.

Dammit. I looked.

Paul and I were walking past Cat and her friends. They were in their usual spot, up on top of the big stairs leading to the school, looking out over all they controlled. And once I started staring, I couldn't stop. Cat looked probably the best I'd ever seen her. She was wearing this black dress with long scraggly black gloves and thick eye makeup. And she was there filming her friends for Coolhunters, with a sweet-looking high-def video cam.

"This is my baby, Kara," she said into the camera as she hugged Kara Privosek. "And this is the honey of all honeys, Rain," she said, pressing her face up to Rain St. James. Then Rain kissed Cat on the lips.

"You're soooooooooo Paris," said Cat. Then she stopped recording and looked down on me. I'd stopped walking and I was standing, staring up at her. Paul tried dragging me away.

Cat looked at me as if I was something bad on the inside of a public toilet.

"Can you perverts stop drooling over us?" she said.

I became conscious again and swallowed hard.

"Sorry," I said, not loud enough to be heard.

Cat whispered into Rain's ear and they laughed at me. Paul started dragging me again.

"Say hi to your dad for us," said Cat, turning back to the group. "Has he used his one phone call yet?"

I stopped.

"C'mon, man," said Paul.

I turned to Cat. Paul had been the only one who'd known about my dad, but Speed had said enough that Cat had put two and two together. It wasn't the first time my dad had been in jail but he'd never been away this long before. He was an activist, Gandhi-style—nonviolent protest. This time he had walked into the Folsom Heights nuclear facility with a bunch of other protestors just to prove how lax security was. The paper said they went right in the front gates past security who didn't even stop them. They climbed a tower and put up a banner that said, NUCLEAR WILL NEVER BE SAFE. Then he was put away, but Mr. Burns and Mr. Smithers inside keep pumping out the radiation. Where's the justice in that? They sentenced him to three months and he'd done a month so far. He told me not to come see him, which sucked. It felt like I hardly ever saw the dude anyway. I was hoping prison might have helped us bond.

Dad was a hero to old-school Kings greenies but the new breed thought he was a wacko and a freeloader. I dug that he stood up for what he believed in but I really didn't want the whole school talking about him getting sent away. I didn't have the kind of rep that could sustain a blow like that.

As I stared at Cat's back, I wanted to say, "You talkin' to me?" and then Paul'd try to drag me off and I'd say it again, "You talkin' to me?" and she'd ignore me. Then I'd unload on her and tell her how stuck-up she was and that everyone despised their group for being so rude to everyone and that her dad had probably done heaps worse things than mine and screwed up the world with his billions of stinkin' plastic coffee cup lids but no one puts people away for that. And I'd tell her I hated the fact that I liked her so much and, anyway, what gave her the right to be so hot?

But I didn't. I just stood there.

Then the bell rang and Cat and her friends all hugged each other. They did this every time they said hello or good-bye. The principal, Mrs. Steele, had actually banned group hugging in the corridors because Cat's group was causing traffic chaos from the science labs all the way down to Woodwork.

Then they left. The whole schoolyard emptied out. Even Paul left. And I just stood there. I felt pretty ordinary.

Just Do It

I flung open the dingy double wooden doors to our workshop—a kind of makeshift shack built by people who clearly hadn't built anything before. The size of a garage, it's where my mom used to paint back in the '80s.

Afternoon sun flooded in, throwing light on thousands of bits of abandoned inventions. A ladder with a missing bottom rung led to a loft where our old creations were kept. What was left of them. Above our workbench there was a shot of me paragliding with Dad when I was ten. Seconds after the photo had been taken I'd nosedived and ripped half the skin off my face. Dad had promised to keep teaching me but he'd been busy changing the world. I'd been trying to get back into the air ever since.

I slammed the package from Speed down on the bench.

"Crack it open," said Paul.

I looked at him.

"No question," he said. "Open it."

It had been the worst day of school ever. Wherever we turned, Cat was filming her friends, flaunting the coolhunting thing in my face and whispering to people, looking my way, and laughing. By the end of the day, I figured our whole year knew about my dad. Everyone was asking what he'd been put away for.

I'd been pretty annoyed all day that I was handing the coolhunting gig and New York to Cat on a platter. But now Paul hated her more than ever and, on the way home, he'd decided that I had to do this thing, with or without him.

I ripped a corner off the packaging, then we both went at it, tearing the wrapping off like three-year-olds at Christmas and throwing it onto the floor. I pulled a pristine high-def video camera, just like Cat's, out of the bigger box. It was slick, black, and very cool. I'd always wanted to make a movie and this camera looked insane. Inside the smaller box was a phone/organizer thing with video-editing software to go with it. We were both pretty crazy for this kind of stuff. Especially me 'cause I'd never had any of it. I just loved the fact that these things hadn't existed until someone looked at a blank piece of paper or a computer screen and had dreamed them up.

"Oh, man, she's so going down," Paul said.

"To Chinatown," I said. "To Chineys, dude."

"Give me a look at that," Paul said, excited, grabbing the phone from me. As he did, he fumbled, dropped it, tried to break the fall with his foot, and kicked it into the metal supports of our workbench. Then it fell to the dirt floor.

"Did that just happen?" I asked him, bending down to pick it up.

The screen had a huge crack in it, a chunk of plastic had fallen out, and the digital display was caked with dirt. I pressed the power button. Nothing.

"Maybe it's not charged," Paul said.

"Maybe you're a moron," I said. "You think that's ever gonna work again?"

Paul looked at it and he knew the answer. "I dunno. They should make them stronger. It was an accident."

I thought about what he'd said for a second and tried not to be angry. I'd never had a cell phone, and to see one given to me and then smashed within ten seconds was pretty hard-core. I clenched a fist and fought hard to resist giving Paul the dead arm to end all dead arms. I sucked a breath in and then uncurled my fingers, leaving nail marks on my palm.

"I guess," I said, tapping the dirt out of the screen. "They should make 'em tougher. Like as if no one's ever going to drop it."

"What's that say?" Paul said.

I grabbed the envelope off the workbench. Inside were instructions scrawled on Coolhunters letterhead.

← THE RULES →

1. Mac, you and Cat will vlog Kings Bay Monday to Friday this week. Tell us something cool you've found, stuff our subscribers won't find anywhere else. Sure, talk to the camera, but show us things as well. People want pictures. Uncover stuff that will blow people away. And if you film or interview anyone, get them to sign a release so you've got the footage rights. (Standard release enclosed.)

2. You will shoot video, cut it on your phone, and upload it to the Coolhunters site by 8:00 p.m. each night. Subscribers will vote overnight and results will be posted on the site at 8:00 a.m. the following day.

3. Win three of the five days and you will become our fifth and final featured coolhunter. You will be paid by us to hunt cool in Kings Bay, to give us feedback on new stuff before it hits the shelves, and to go on international coolhunts. The first is in New York in a month's time. I fly out to the Great Barrier Reef Monday morning but text me at 212 555 2635 if you want to play ball. Otherwise I'll pick up the camera at the end of the week.

"Almost too good to be true," I said.

Paul busted his cell out of his pocket. "Want to tell 'em you're in?"

I grabbed his phone and punched Speed's digits.

"Wish I could do this on my own phone," I said.

"Phone, schmone. We're goin' to New York, man," said Paul.

"New freakin' York," I said with a huge grin.

Game On

Paul and I powered down Herriman Street toward the beach—me pedaling, Paul in the aluminum sidecar with the Perspex windshield we'd made. The sidecar had pedals inside so we could ride twice as fast as an ordinary bike, but without looking like total losers on a tandem. In fact, it looked pretty cool. One of the many vehicles we'd invented.

The only problem with it was that there was a steering wheel in the sidecar linked to my handlebars, so when I wanted to go right and Paul wanted to go left, the strongest man won, i.e., me. But being stronger than Paul was nothing to boast about. His arms got tired grating cheese.

We took a right on Hutchence and booted it toward Main Beach where it was widely known that cool people hung out. Paul and I rarely went there but I guess we had to get with the program if we were gonna hunt cool for a living.

In the park in front of the beach we could see a bunch of metalcore music fans with their Parkway Drive T-shirts and facial bruises from stage diving. There were two guys wearing Oakland Raiders tops with caps on sideways and bandannas around their necks. There were lifeguards zincing up for an afternoon on the beach. There were rich families strolling the path in their Polo gear, licking choc-chip and super-fudge chunk. There were loved-up ferals on the grass sucking face and two yummy mommies pushing thousand-dollar prams full of sleeping, vomiting, pooping kids. But you couldn't call it cool.

"This is rash," said Paul.

"It's raccoon dung with butts," I said.

"It's itchy legs and shrimps."

We did this from time to time—came up with words that felt like what we were trying to say without actually making any sense. But we knew what we meant.

In the middle of it all we saw Cat cruising solo on old-school skates wearing pulled-up rainbow-stripe socks, yellow hot pants, big sunglasses, a wild, colored hair-extension thing, and a lollipop in her mouth. We stood and watched as she filmed some guy's haircut, a dude's shoes, the way a Japanese kid was carrying his phone, two dudes wearing black nail polish, and then some guy's butt. As we rode closer, I realized it was his lower back that she was interested in. On it was a tattoo with some kind of wings.

"What is that? Like, a flying butt?" asked Paul.

We pulled up next to Cat just as she finished shooting the

butt. He was a hip-hop dude with big silver headphones, tracksuit, Adidas no laces.

"Thanks, babe," she said. "Check it out on the Web tonight." Then she got the guy to sign a release and gave him what looked like a little Coolhunters business card. She must have made it herself. She didn't waste any time.

I wanted to look busy so I pulled out the camera and started filming two seven-year-old boys dressed as pirates trying to rip each other's ears off over near the playground slide.

Cat went to skate off, saw us, and did a double take, braking with her toe-stopper.

"What do you think you're doing?" she asked.

I stopped recording.

"Oh, Cat, hi," Paul said, trying to act casual. "Don't you know? Yeah, Mac's doin' the trial. I thought Speed would've texted you. That's pretty rude of him actually, 'cause—"

"What?"

"Yeah, he gave us a camera," Paul said. "Nice, too. If you use the night mode in the day you can see through people's clothes, so watch out," he lied, grabbing the camera and pointing it at Cat. She tried to cover herself, not knowing whether to believe him.

"Yeah, we've shot some incredible stuff," he went on. "You should log on tonight and check it out. Might learn a thing or two about cool. Nice socks, by the way."

Cat suddenly looked self-conscious of her knee-highs and I

couldn't help but smile. They did look pretty ridiculous. Even if they were wrapped around the best legs in Kings Bay.

"Did you get a cell, too?" she asked.

I glared at Paul.

"Yeah. Sure we did," I said.

"You guys bailed. You can't run away like babies and then change your mind and come back."

"Can and have," said Paul.

Cat stared at us. I always felt kind of like a different species when she did that, like she could send us to the pound or have the ranger fine us for being in an area where only humans were allowed.

"Well, I guess it's kind of easier to beat you two geeks than, say, anyone else in town who might have trialed," she said, gazing all around, looking for her next conquest. A guy came up behind her and kissed her on the neck. It was Egg, the football guy who'd been lying under the jump on Sunday afternoon. I didn't know what his real name was. There was a rumor that he had tackled a kid at his last school so hard that the kid had been in the hospital for two months. But some people said it was just a rumor that Egg spread to make kids scared of him. Whatever. It worked.

"You nearly left tire marks on me yesterday. I ought to pound you," he said, smiling.

"These rejects are trialing for Coolhunters," Cat said to Egg.

"What?" he said, laughing.

"Yeah." She laughed too. "Look, you guys should probably know that I don't like to be beaten. Fact, I hate it. I definitely plan to be in New York and I will do what it takes. This is my dream job and if you get in my way I'll have someone go postal on you, 'kay?"

Paul and I both looked up at Egg. We were guessing that he was the postman. He smiled, flashing a gap with a missing tooth, and then dragged the roller-derby queen off along the path toward the old shipwreck on Samsara Beach.

"Well," said Paul.

"She's so cute," I said.

"Will you shut up? She's the devil's spawn, the enemy. You'd better realize that if we're gonna win this thing."

Paul and I scanned the beachfront, totally underwhelmed by it all. Where Cat saw winged butts and elbow piercings, we saw nothing. I guess you had to have an eye for this stuff. Or at least care about it. All we could see was a whole pile of lame. But if we didn't shoot something, we were going down.

The First VLOG

"It's a world capital of cool. Home to celebrities, surfers, and skinny models from LA. Kings Bay is comin' atcha with me, Mac Slater, hunting all the hottest stuff and servin' it up daily—"

I stopped and hung my head. We were down on Main Beach—Paul shooting, me hosting, the lighthouse in the distance behind me.

"What?" said Paul. "That one was good."

"I can't say this stuff," I said.

"What? You need to know what your motivation is?" Paul said, eyes drooping. "Your motivation is I'm gonna kill you if you don't get it right. It's nearly dark and we've done, like, two thousand takes of this. I gotta go to my sister's thingo at school later, so shut up and talk."

"You got a real way of nurturing a performance," I said.

"Ever thought about a career as a director?"

"And, go!" said Paul.

I took a deep breath. "It's a world capital of cool. Home to celebrities, surfers, and skinny models from . . ."

⊲ Upload ⊳

7:57 p.m. "I just want to watch it one last time," I said.

"You can, but it'll mean we don't get it in by eight. Which might actually be a good thing," Paul said.

We were surrounded by a bunch of travelers with dirty hair and tie-dyed T-shirts in the Arts Village Backpacker Café. Paul had cut our first piece on iMovie. He was trying to make up for totaling the organizer/phone thing. A German guy next to us said, "I see it is looking pretty good, *ja*?"

"Mac, I'm going to need that computer at eight," said Mr. Kim, walking past with a coffee order.

"Yeah, all right," I said. "Do it."

Paul hit "Upload."

I covered my face with my hands and peeked through a crack. There was me onscreen, standing on the beach with the lighthouse in the background. "It's a world capital of cool. Home to . . ."

As if the lighthouse was cool. And then we had footage

of all these kooks on the beachfront with strips of eyebrow hair missing and chicks wearing knee-high biker boots in the middle of summer. Some guy had *Mom* tattooed across his arm and we shot that and stuck it in. I mean it was kind of funny-cool and I think he meant it as a joke, but who knew? There was a Japanese girl wearing a Nike hoodie, Gucci shades, and a crown on her head. An old dude with curly gray hair, a straw hat, and a Grateful Dead T-shirt. A golden retriever leaping a yard into the air to catch a funky pink tennis ball and a homeless guy sleeping on a canvas bag with a lemonade bottle leaning against a post next to him. None of it was cool to us but it's what we'd seen. It was just the reality.

Then suddenly it was all over. I was tired and hungry and I felt even less cool than I had before I became a coolhunter.

"It'll be right," I said, lying.

"Rockin'," said Paul. "Three of the lamest minutes of video ever committed to the Web."

I looked at him. Even that word—*rockin'*—was so not cool. Man, we sucked.

We grabbed our things and an Indian chick with a little bindi between her eyes nabbed our seat and started Bebo-ing. We walked off down the path toward the bus without saying a word.

We stopped at our workshop. There was a scooter leaning against the side. Paul grabbed it. "I don't know if I'm gonna come tomorrow," I said.

"You'll be there," he said. "It's like roadkill. How can you not want to see it? Meet me, ten to eight at the corner."

And he rode off along the wooden walkway that cut through the ti-tree lake and into the night.

Tuesday

I slopped rice milk into a bowl, wolfed three scoops of oats, grabbed my bag, and leaped down the steps of our bus. I was feeling a bunch better this morning.

"Gotta bolt, Ma," I said.

"Slow down. Did you have herbs in your juice?"

"I gotta get to school," I said.

"It's not even eight. What's the rush?" she asked. She was sitting outside in the sun in a yoga pose, eating sprouted bread— this weird uncooked stuff that takes like a thousand chews to get through.

"I'll make you a sandwich," she said.

"Please not with that bread," I said.

"What's wrong with it?"

I usually ate all the kooky stuff she served up but since we'd started on the raw food thing—yep, nothing cooked— dining at our place had really gone downhill. We hadn't eaten a scrap of cooked food at home in nearly a year. I sometimes ate normal food when I was out in the world but there was no way I could break that to my mom. Let me tell you, though, there's a reason why humans actually cook bread.

"I'm doing the coolhunting thing," I said as I kissed her and grabbed my in-line board. It was a two-wheel skateboard that Paul and I had been working on. We figured it'd be quicker to build our own board than to save for one. But we were still having a couple of little teething problems. Like wiping out every five yards.

"What?" she said. "Mac, hold on a moment. I thought you'd—"

"Yeah, well, I changed my mind. See, Cat, the girl who . . ." I thought for a second about all my reasons for wanting to do this and I knew she'd talk me out of it. "Doesn't matter," I said. "I'm just doing it. It'll be all right."

"But who are these men? And why do they want you to do this? I've heard the Internet can be really dangerous for—"

"Ma, it's fine. Really. It's just a trial. Don't worry about it. I've got to go check and see if we won."

"Won what?"

But I was off up the path.

"Mac?" she called. "I've got something for you."

I turned, expecting her to be offering a kiss, which she knew was banned in public. But she had something in her hand. I walked back to her.

"It's a feather I found. Thought it might help with your flying."

I smiled and took the feather. It glinted blue when I tilted it into the light. I poked it into the front pocket of my bag so it was sticking out a little. It looked good. Sure, maybe it wouldn't make me fly, but I needed all the help I could get.

"Thanks, Ma. I'll talk to you tonight. And relax. It's cool."

I skated through reception and out to the road before wiping out. I was really starting to get the hang. I jumped back on and skated hard for school, crossing my fingers all the way.

And the winner is . . .

We knew the result as soon as we rolled through the gate.

It was seven minutes past eight, seven minutes since the results had been posted online, and Cat's crew were group hugging at the top of the big steps. But it wasn't just the ordinary hug. It was like a group hug–jump–squeal thing. Then it broke and they all kind of swizzled their fingers together in the middle and then went back into the hug. Cat was too cool for squealing and swizzling so she just stood there and let them worship her.

"Do you think she won?" Paul asked, deadpan, jumping off his skatey.

"Dunno. They look pretty upset," I said, picking up my board and folding it in the middle.

We shuffled slowly toward them. Kids everywhere were looking at me. Staring. They stopped and watched as we went past. Someone on the basketball court yelled out, "Loser!" Other kids just had this look of pity in their eyes.

Clearly Cat had spread the word to everyone about the trial.

"Man, it's cool being a celebrity," I said.

"You wanna go see how bad the damage is?" Paul asked in a low voice.

"Not really," I muttered back.

We kept our heads down and tried to slide past without some sarcastic comment from Cat. She saw me but she didn't say anything. Just gave me this look that said, "You never had a chance." It was like she thought she'd won the whole thing. We made it to the bottom of the steps and ducked into the library.

"Two minutes for computers," called Mrs. Roberts, the librarian, once we were inside. "Two more minutes only. We have a three-unit economics class coming in early."

I sat at a computer and took a breath. I still wasn't sure if I wanted to see.

"What're you doin', man?" Paul snapped.

"I just—"

Paul leaned over my shoulder and googled "Coolhunters," then clicked through.

On the home page there were pics of the four chosen hunters, then an image of Cat and one of me, taken from our vlogs. I had a weird look on my face like I was straining to push something out.

Paul clicked "See Who Won!" The page took forever to load. Four seconds of hell. Then BANG. Right there. Cat had 35,422 votes. Paul and I had 736. She had slain us by nearly 35,000 votes.

"I didn't think it'd be this bad," I said.

"I did," said Paul.

"Thanks."

The comments left were pretty ferocious, too:

Is this guy some kind of joke? For a second I thought I was on uncoolhunters.com.
—Fashionista, Boone, NC, U.S.A.

mac is whack
—Thunderbutt, Melbourne, Australia

whats tha deal? i swear i saw a tshirt this guy coolhunted in kmart. is that the most original thing comin outta kings bay?
—FraidyCat4, Seattle, U.S.A.

A dog catching a ball? This is cool? I give my vote definitely to the girl
—Antoine, Marrakech, Morocco

It turned out to be the hottest day of the year so far. But not so hot for me. Cat and her friends must have told everyone in school to watch the Coolhunters trial unfold.

In the hallways, kids were giving me hell, calling me the uncool hunter and telling me to give up. I was waiting for someone to stick a KICK ME sign on my back.

The emos; the basketball guys; even the heavy metal dudes with long gray jackets, straggly facial hair, and knuckles decked with silver rings were muttering and mocking me as I walked past their wall. Ryan Morphett and Chris Brown were the geekiest dudes in our year and they were lovin' it. I was taking the heat off them, and their zits were popping with excitement. Paul and I had met at the same spot every lunchtime for nearly two years but today he wasn't there. He made out later like he'd been looking for me but I knew he was trying to distance himself from the great coolhunting disaster. So there I was, alone, sitting outside the bathroom near biology surrounded by the stench and sound of people emptying their bowels. I had no money to buy food and I would have given my left thumb for one of those uncooked bread sandwiches.

Cat, rather than rub it in, had gone back to pretending I didn't exist, which is the way it had always been between us. I thought about her every third minute and I didn't even rate a blip on her radar. I didn't know which was worse—her venting bile on me or ignoring me altogether.

"Hey," said a voice. It was Jewels. She had her hair up in all these little blue pig-tail things. She sat next to me on the bench. "Whatcha doin'?"

"Just hangin' with my friends," I said. She laughed.

"You want my TVP sandwich?" she asked, a grin on her face.

TVP was the most sickening substance on earth. Texturized Vegetable Protein. A vegetarian meat substitute that tasted and looked like vomit.

"Has it got ketchup?"

She laughed again, took it out of her bag, and gave it to me.

"Don't listen to what everyone's saying," she said.

"A little hard not to. I didn't even want to do this stupid thing anyway. They just asked me and I wanted to beat Cat and . . ."

"It sounds pretty good," she said. "Traveling and all that."

"Yeah," I said and took a bite, trying to tell myself it was something tastier. Like pus.

"Well," she said. "I don't think you're a loser. You can come hang with me and Im if you like."

"Nah." She and her friend Imogen were obsessed with this pop band and that's all they talked about all day long. I didn't know if I could hack listening to a debate about what some Dutch girl had written on the band's MySpace the night before.

"No, really, you should come," she said. "I promise we won't—"

"No. I'm fine. Leave me alone!" I said, probably a little too harshly.

Jewels stood up. "Okay. Sit there by yourself with your TVP, you winner," she said and walked off.

So I sat there till the bell. Even with the taste of that sandwich and the sweet perfume drifting out of the men's bathroom, I was too depressed to move.

After school, Paul wasn't in the usual spot. I saw him hurrying off with Nick Jones and Bradley Farrar, the guys he hung out with sometimes to talk sci-fi 'cause I seriously couldn't provide that service. I chucked my board down and dug in. I had to tell him that the whole coolhunting gig was over. I'd had enough humiliation for one lifetime. It was either give up the trial or change schools. Maybe both. But I couldn't take another four days of this.

Thunder groaned overhead. Dark clouds were gathering out over the beach. They looked kind of green, like we were in for hail, even.

As I skated, I realized that maybe I'd gone into this whole thing for the wrong reasons. I wanted to try to beat Cat, to take revenge on her maybe, for ignoring me for so long. And I wanted to go to New York and to give this coolhunting thing a shot. But why did I think it was possible to beat her when Cat was already cool? Then, yesterday, Paul and I had just gone out and filmed what we thought other people might think was cool because we didn't believe the stuff we liked was cool enough.

"Hey man, why didn't you wait?" I said to Paul, skating up behind him. "We've got work."

Paul and the guys went from laughing and talking about space ninjas or something dumb to giving me these looks that said, *What do you think you're doing?*

Paul said, "Well, if you're gonna skate ahead, I'll just meet you there, okay?"

I thought he was joking at first. Then I realized he wasn't. The other guys shared a look that told me to disappear. So I did.

Purgatory

We knew there was something very wrong going down, even from around the corner. The other guys had peeled off home on the edge of town so I'd dropped back, and Paul and I were walking together. He still wasn't talking to me. Until this: "What is that smell?"

The air was hot from the day and a stink hit us like a hard slap. The guys' toilets smelled like cinnamon doughnuts next to this.

"I don't know. Is it, like . . . maybe someone died?"

"Is it the chicken factory?" Paul asked.

We took a left into the alley behind Taste Sensation, the two-bit burger joint where we held down McJobs as kitchen hands/front-counter dudes for five-fiddy an hour one after-noon a week. It was a try-hard franchise store with one out-let, right here on the main street of Kings. The worst food in town, but someone had to feed the backpackers.

Thunder moaned all around. As we climbed the concrete

stairs to the kitchen, we realized exactly what the stench was. A thick sludge flowed out from underneath the screen door. And then the door was flung open. "Get in here and help. NOW!" yelled Mr. Dykstra, our boss. Dykstra had a thick mustache, a fear of spending money, and an attitude.

Paul and I stepped inside, Paul dancing to one side, trying not to get his shoes gooed. The whole kitchen floor was covered with fat and three-week-old, chewed-up food—skanky lettuce leaves, chunks of decaying beefburger, warm tuna, and bits of egg.

"The grease trap," Dykstra shrieked. "It exploded."

The grease trap was a filter. All restaurants have them. Everything that goes down the sink passes through it to stop bad stuff from getting into the drains. And, at Taste Sensation, this meant some very bad stuff. It was supposed to be emptied by professionals once every few weeks but Mr. Dykstra was so cheap, he emptied it himself. And sometimes he forgot.

Imagine the worst thing you've ever smelled in your life. And then multiply it by four thousand and you have the smell of an exploding grease trap. The filth was erupting from a cupboard in the wall, flowing in all directions, and heading toward the dining area. Dykstra raced out to explain to a couple of remaining customers.

"Please accept our apologies. Taste Sensation will be back to normal soon. Would you like a pass for a free kebab?" said Mr. Dykstra, but they were gone.

"Go!" he spat at me and Paul. "Get on it! Scoop it into the tin drum."

Paul and I jumped, scared of being canned from our high-paying jobs, I guess. We ripped off our shoes and I waded into the pool of wrongness, heading for the big tin drum in the corner. Paul was still dancing from foot to foot at the edge of the flow.

"What're you doing?" I asked.

"I can't do this. I'm worried about my allergies, y'know," he said.

"Get over here now or you're gonna eat it," I said.

"I'd better not get a rash," he said as he took his first step, hand clamped to his nose like a mask. Then another step. The fat lapped up to his ankles. He groaned loudly.

"This is cool. Should have brought the camera," I said.

"Probably cooler than what we shot yesterday," Paul replied through his cupped hand.

The stench made me gag, and I only just managed to hold on to my lunch. I slid the empty drum along the floor into the middle of the goop and grabbed two buckets from under the sink, tossing one to Paul. It splashed into the fat pool.

Mr. Dykstra was on the phone out in the alley, walking in circles.

We started bucketing.

"This is the worst day of my life," I said.

Paul didn't say anything.

"Why'd you ditch me at school?" I asked him.

"I didn't," he said. "I couldn't find you."

"That's strange," I said. "You've never had trouble finding me before."

I filled my bucket. It had something floating in it that looked suspiciously like a decaying rat.

Paul was quiet and drizzled a tiny quarter-bucketful into the drum.

"So, why?" I said.

Paul paused for a second. "This coolhunting thing sucks. I think we should pull out," he said.

"Right," I said, pouring in another bucket. "Yesterday you didn't want me to do it because you couldn't do it with me. And today—"

"Well, as if we're ever going to beat her," he said. I knew it was true and it was how I felt too, but his negativity was getting on my nerves.

"Why not?" I asked.

Paul looked around. "Do you have eyes?" he said. "And a nose? You think Cat's somewhere across town in another gross diner knee-deep in regurgitated blurk? No. We are not cool, Mac, and we never will be, so why humiliate ourselves?"

"Don't talk. Work!" yelled Dykstra through the back screen door. "You want me to lose more customers?" Then he went back to his phone conversation.

"See what I mean?" Paul whispered.

We worked silently for an hour, scooping, mopping, and wiping till every drop of gunk was gone. I spent the time stewing about what Paul had said. Knowing he was right but not wanting him to be. Then we re-opened the place and did an hour working the counter and deep fryer. I was scared of how long that oil had been in there. A storm warning came through on the radio, the first big one of the season.

Dykstra appeared through the back door right at five o'clock and said, "Good boys. Very good. Let me pay you now for today."

He went to the cash register and he gave us eleven bucks each. I had to peel my crusty fingers apart to get the money into my pocket.

"See you next week," he said.

"Not if I can help it," I said under my breath as we headed for the door. Paul and I stepped out onto the main street.

It was raining. We stood there, getting wet, letting the goop wash off us, looking like pigs. Two girls from the seventh grade passed by, staring at us and laughing. Paul wiped some fat off his leg and flicked it at them, and they scurried away.

"Man, I love being a coolhunter," I said.

A couple of flashes of lightning made everything white for a second or two. Then another flash exploded over the lighthouse in the distance.

I washed some more fat out of my eyebrows and hair in the rain.

"Lightning," I said to Paul.

Another flash.

"So what," he said, not knowing what I was getting at.

A boom of thunder and more lightning. I stepped back, trying to get a better look at the lighthouse between the buildings across the street.

"You know what I'm thinking?" I asked.

"What're you thinking?" he said.

I raised my brows and he knew what I meant.

"Oh, no way."

"What would you rather do? Win this thing and get paid to hunt cool or spend the rest of your life working here?" I asked him, starting to walk away.

"Your dad won't even be there," he said.

"Don't care," I said. "Let's go, before the storm ends."

"I said I was quitting."

"Fine, then. Quit."

And I was gone.

⊲ Race Through ⊳ Rain

Lightning erupted all around and wind screamed in my face. The sun set pretty late at this time of year but the cloud cover was making everything look grim. Cars flicked past in both directions, lights on, as I charged along the edge of the road on my bike. I looked over my shoulder. Paul was close behind. His retirement from coolhunting had lasted about fifteen seconds. He couldn't handle the thought of me doing something fun alone. So we'd gone back to the workshop and grabbed two old BMX bikes we'd found at the dump and the camera, which was now in my backpack. I was praying the pack was waterproof as we charged up the winding Lighthouse Road.

A car honked loudly, telling us to get out of the way. I guess they could barely see us now, with the rain falling in thick gray sheets. Standard pre-summer weather in Kings. Hotter than hell in the day and then the skies crack around five with a killer storm. Clear again by seven.

Paul yelled out: "Is this stupid to be riding metal bikes in a storm?"

I didn't answer. A car swished past and sprayed us. There was an old sign up ahead that pointed one way to the lighthouse and another way to Rainbow Creek. I took the Rainbow turnoff and I felt a lump in my stomach. I hadn't been up to my dad's place in months.

As we neared the top of the hill, the storm was right over us and my calves were on fire. I powered on toward Dad's, wondering if anyone would think his lightning farm was as cool as I did.

Lightning made massive fractures in the sky and thunder exploded on top of it. The earth trembled. Paul and I dumped our bikes at the fence and bolted toward the old sheep-shearing lean-to. Adrenaline sped through me as we ran the final few yards into the open-sided shed, gulping great lungfuls of air. The rain hammered on the tin roof above.

I busted out the camera and dragged an old sawhorse over to use as a tripod. Paul set it up. I looked at the open field in front of us. There were four hundred metal rods, each about two yards high, sticking out of the ground in an area of three miles by one. It looked like a gigantic bed of nails. My dad reckoned this was his life's great work. His lightning farm. All the energy hitting the poles was sent to a huge aluminum shed a few hundred yards to our right. The problem was that most of the power couldn't be stored. It had to be used right away and they wouldn't let

Dad send his energy into the electricity grid. Too high-voltage or something. Dad said his alternative energy would save the world. Most people said he was a dreamer. Or worse.

He'd been traveling in America when he was twenty-something and got inspired by some dude's sculpture in a field in New Mexico. It was called Lightning Field and it looked just like Dad's farm does now. Dad had this dream that if he could harness all the energy in those lightning strikes, he could power Kings Bay and the surrounding towns forever. He'd been working on it for twenty years.

Paul hit the record button on the camera and we watched as massive bolts of electricity slammed into the poles. Paul's glasses glowed. The explosions were almost nuclear.

"Pretty cool, huh?" I yelled to Paul.

He just stood there, mouth open, blown away. He'd been up here before in a storm, but nothing like this. Usually, we were lucky to see a single rod get struck.

"Cooler than shooting feral people making out and butt tattoos on the beach," I yelled.

I checked my watch. It was 5:37. We still had time to make the eight p.m. deadline.

"We're so gonna win tomorrow," I said.

Paul was busy watching the show on the camera flip screen, but he knew it too.

As another bolt of lightning struck I saw a figure dart out of the shed to our right. It was heading toward a houseboat another forty yards away. There was a dim light on inside the boat. The figure wore a Driza-Bone coat and wide-brim hat.

"You see that?" Paul asked.

He knew I did. "He's supposed to be away for another two months," I said. So either someone else was up here or my dad had been released. The knot in my stomach tightened. I hadn't seen him since before he went in. He hadn't wanted me to. But I wanted to see him now.

A great white crack split the sky in two.

"Let's go," I shouted over the sound of the rain. I grabbed the camera and threw it into my backpack.

"Where we going?" Paul asked.

"Dad's," I screamed back.

"No. Why? Hang on," he said.

I ran out of the shed, Paul following closely behind. We bolted around the edge of the field, staying as far from the rods as we could.

Huge puddles had formed everywhere and we galloped through them. Up ahead I could see the houseboat. My dad had started building the thing out of used boat parts about ten years ago, just after my mom left him. It had been moored at a marine junkyard on the edge of town but even they evicted him, saying the thing was an eyesore. So now it sat up here on the hill, half-finished, with my dad camping inside. Lightning above made the boat glow white hot for a second. Paul and I cranked up the speed.

"Ru-u-u-u-u-u-n!" I screamed, like that was helpful.

Out of the corner of my eye I saw a bolt zap a nearby rod. Another fifty meters down a gravel path, we hit the boat's rope ladder, climbed it, and pounded on the rusty iron door. I waited nervously, out of breath, ready to surprise my dad.

Brian Slater

The door opened just a little and a heavily bearded face peered out.

"Dad! It's me. Me and Paul. Can we come in?" There was a slight pause before the chain came off the door and my dad, dressed in his usual jeans and checked lumberjack shirt, opened up.

"What're you doin' 'ere?" he asked.

"What are *you* doing here?" I asked him back. "You didn't escape, did you?" He didn't seem to be wearing an orange jumpsuit or to have a cannonball chained to his ankle.

He shut the door behind us and grunted. He was a big bear of a man, my dad. Came from a long line of bears. He towered over me and Paul. Grunted a lot too.

"What're you doing out in a storm? Get yourself killed running through these rods," he said.

"We were filming. When did you get out? Why didn't you tell me?" I asked.

He coughed up something thick and headed toward the kitchen.

"Can I get you something?"

Paul didn't say anything.

"Maybe juice," I said.

"No juice. Tea. I'll get you tea. Wait 'ere," he said.

My eyes darted around the small living area. It was lit by a single bare bulb, and one wall of the room was just a tarpaulin. There were books everywhere. Hundreds of them in piles all around the room, piles that had tipped over, covering almost every square inch of floor. There was lots of equipment, too—generator parts, a stack of spare lightning rods in one corner. There were failed electrical gadgets, inventions never completed. One of my dad's big regrets was that he'd never finished anything in his life. He had tons of ideas but he wasn't a big closer. There was a staircase opposite the door leading down to my dad's bedroom in the belly of the boat. I could see piles of paper at the bottom of the stairs, thousands of pages of his unfinished thesis on lightning farming.

Paul looked a bit freaked by the place. He hadn't been here in years. It was a bit creepy, I guess. We went and sat on the edge of an old daybed with an orange cover—the one I had slept on back when I used to stay at Dad's on weekends. His giant dogs,

Louis and Edison, took up the rest of the bed. They were Great Danes crossed with something else big. Horses, maybe. Getting them off the boat for a walk had always been hell. I wondered who had looked after them while Dad was away. I imagined them in the cell with him. I noticed he hadn't asked me to take care of them. *Thanks, Pops.* Edison looked scared, eyes flicking around as lightning lit up the room in explosive bursts. Louis was sleeping and snoring so loud it almost drowned out the sound of rain on the tin roof.

It was a bit embarrassing bringing Paul here. His house was weird in its own way, but nothing like this. I started to wonder if we should leave just as Dad emerged from the kitchen with two cups of tea in dirty mugs. One had "No Nukes" on the side. The other had "TCB" and a lightning bolt. Dad was an Elvis fan and "TCB" was the King's logo. It stood for "Takin' Care of Business." I secretly didn't mind a bit of Elvis, but it wasn't something I was proud of.

"No sugar," said Dad. "But it's good tea. Organic. Friend of mine grows it down the road. Full of antioxidants."

Then he coughed again, nearly barking up a lung into Paul's mug. Not a great ad for antioxidants.

"You okay?" I asked.

"Yeah, got this rotten flu," he said, flopping into his old green velvet armchair, caked in dog hair.

"Right." I really wanted to talk to him about prison, but what do you ask your old man when he gets out of the big house? How was the food? Were the people nice? Did you think of your son once the whole time? And you never knew with my dad. He'd either talk your ears off for an hour or he'd grunt and get annoyed. I decided to go for it anyway.

"How was it?" I asked.

He didn't respond.

"Dad?" I said, louder, thinking he mustn't have heard me over the snoring and rain.

"How was what?"

"Well, the past month. When'd you get out?" I asked.

"A week ago."

"Why didn't you call?"

"Because you'd start asking me questions," he said, grabbing a mug from a pile of books next to his chair.

"Right," I said. "Does that mean you don't want to talk about it?"

He took a long sip and wiped the tea from his mustache.

Paul didn't say anything. He looked afraid of the brown marks around the rim of his mug and the big milk lumps floating on top of his tea. Paul's mom cleaned their place like it was a hospital and Paul had serious issues with grime. Neither of us liked hot drinks so we just held them. We were still dripping all over the place.

"I wanted to talk to you. About the farm," I said.

"What do you want to know?" he asked, leaning forward into the light. He didn't look any different from how he did before he went away. No number tattooed on his arm. He had dark rings under his eyes and his hair and beard were wild, but that was nothing new. I looked at my watch. 6:31 p.m.

"See, we're doing this thing called Coolhunters," I said, "where we film stuff and put it on the Web and if we win this trial we'll go to New York and they'll pay us and . . ." I knew he wasn't following any of it so I cut to the chase.

"Anyway, we filmed the farm and I want to interview you. Is that okay?"

"Why?"

"Well, it'd just really help for people to know a bit about lightning farming and all that," I said.

Dad stood up and patted his hair down.

"How do I look?"

"Good, Dad, you look fine. You can sit down. We'll do it in your chair."

Paul gave me a sideways *Is he for real?* look. I ignored it.

Dad sat down and Paul grabbed the camera from my bag, propping it on a pile of books on the desk next to us. He used a nearby dog towel to wipe rain off the camera, then stabbed the record button with his thumb.

"Okay," I said, "can you just tell us how you came up with the idea of the lightning farm in the first place?"

"Well," he said, adjusting himself in his chair, "I was traveling in the Southwest of the States twenty or so years ago. . . ."

Dad spat out the whole history of his idea, the challenges,

the wildest storms, the fires from blown-up transformers, and the naysayers who still believe it'll never work. Once he got started, there was no stopping him.

"It'll change the world, you see. A simple matter of, of drawing on one of nature's most powerful renewable resources and directing that energy into the power grid. In twenty years' time they'll be everywhere, lightning farms. Trouble is trying to get your snout in the tiny trough of, of money to develop this stuff, of course."

I looked at my watch. Six forty-seven. I needed him to wind down.

"So, what's the secret to getting alternative ideas like this out there?" I asked him.

He sat there for a moment, combing his beard with his fingers.

"Follow your bliss," he said. "Do what you love. No matter what they say. Other people will want you to go on their trip but you got to do what's in your gut. 'No' and 'impossible' have to be wiped from your vocabulary. Stick-to-it-iveness they call it." He sat there for a long moment like he was going to say something else, and then he said: "Is that enough? I'm all talked out. Rain's eased. How 'bout you boys get goin'?"

Juiced

7:13 p.m. Paul and I charged down Lighthouse Road. Juiced. The storm was over but strong winds were coming in off the water, blowing us all over the road. The occasional car whipped by on the dark, wet roadway. Lightning made clouds glow on the horizon. The lighthouse's beam swept around over our heads.

Forty-seven minutes to cut and upload the video. I had a pretty good idea of the best bits of Dad's interview and I was replaying the blasts of lightning from the farm over and over in my head, imagining Dad's words with lightning pictures. But another idea was niggling away at the back of my mind.

"You know what would be really cool?" I called out to Paul, dropping back to ride side by side with him.

"What?"

"If we could get the bike back in the air by the end of the week."

Paul grinned. "You kidding me?"

"No. For Friday's vlog. Go out with a bang."

"That's only three days away," Paul said.

"I know," I said as we turned away from the beach and started charging down Messenger Street toward the Arts Village.

"That's the best thing I've ever heard," Paul said.

⊲ Cat Tells All ⊳

We'd uploaded our lightning piece by five to eight. I didn't even watch it once we'd cut it. I knew how good it was. The lightning looked awesome and my dad had said some pretty cool stuff. As soon as it was up, we watched Cat's vlog. It was a video fashion piece. She'd gotten Kara to interview her on the beachfront and Cat wore a different outfit for each question. It was pretty pathetic. But I still watched it. Twice. Here's some of it:

Kara's voice offscreen: Cat DeVrees, describe your personal style.

Cat: Right now I'd say it's, like, lollipop princess. Other times it's been, like, a hot rodeo/trailer-trash thing. And then I've been through the whole punk look but I gave my punk a kind of Paris café twist, y'know, rather than a funky seventies feel.

(Cat changes outfit.)

Kara: How many pairs of shoes do you have?

Cat: Do I have to be honest? If I do, I would have to say about two, no, maybe three hundred. It's kind of embarrassing but I just never know what to wear. Shoes and bags are my life. I would be dead without shoes.

(Cat changes again.)

Kara: What perfume do you use?

Cat: I'm totally D & G right now.

(And again.)

Kara: What hair do you want that you can't have?

Cat: Um. Red. Like, carroty orange. Redheads are so cool. And freckles and glasses, too. God, freckles are divine. I'm so jealous of red hair and freckles. I mean, not if you were born with them. But for a party or something. I would totally love that.

(Change.)

Kara: Who would you dress like if you could dress like anyone?

Cat: Anyone? I would say like Cat DeVrees. Because I've got a hot look and I'm very photogenic.

(Changes again.)

Kara: Who would you like to spend a week on a desert island with?

Cat: Again, I would say Cat DeVrees. You have no idea how funny I can be when I want to be.

Kara: Yeah, but who would you tell the jokes to?

Cat: Oh, yeah. Well, I don't know, I guess I'd have to ask someone else along. But I'd prefer it was just me.

(Change.)

Kara: What's your fave style site right now?

Cat: TheSartorialist.com and Video.Style.com.

(Change.)

Kara: How are you dressing for the party of the year, Friday night?

Cat: Zen. With a rock edge.

ReaL Inventors

8:12 p.m. I pulled open the double doors of our workshop and jumped on the bike to crank up our light. A few years back we'd built a bike that powered a light globe. The paper did a story on it. The coolest thing was that you only had to ride for a couple of minutes to charge a battery that gave you nearly an hour's light.

Tonight I was psyched and I pedaled fast. The light was glowing bright. I had to hold myself back so I didn't generate too much wattage and blow the globe again. Paul climbed up the old wooden ladder with the missing bottom rung that led to the loft. He started pulling down the bike frame that I'd totaled two days earlier.

"Do what's in your gut. Stick-to-it-iveness," Paul mumbled to no one in particular as he climbed down, lowering the frame to the ground. "That was so cool. Even though your dad's old, he kind of knows stuff. I mean, what if he really does bring lightning to the masses? They'll give him the Nobel, man. Sincerely. When people see our vlog, maybe someone'll give him money. I mean, if he doesn't end up back in prison."

Paul looked at me. He knew he'd said a stupid thing as soon as it had come out. I still felt weird about the whole thing.

"I'm sorry, man—"

"Naaaah, forget about it," I said, pretending I wasn't really hurt, putting my head down as I pedaled.

"No, really, I—"

"Naaah, man, it's good," I said. "I hope your old man stays out of the hole too. Although I don't think they put you in prison for being the most boring dude ever born," I said.

"Oh, right," said Paul. "Well, do they imprison mothers for never holding down a real job and spending their whole lives twirling flaming batons and making batons that no one buys?"

The idea of this game was really to cut as close to the bone as possible. Cruel but funny.

"I don't know," I replied. "Do they put mothers away for covering the couch and all the walkways in the house with plastic in case someone actually enjoys themselves for once?" Paul rushed me, gave me a crow-peck on the head, and retreated fast, so I jumped off the bike and tackled him to the dirt floor of the workshop.

"Get off, idiot. Owwwww," he whined.

"Take it back," I said, digging my fingers into his ribs.

"Take what back?" he said. He was in the kind of pain that made him laugh.

I pushed him down and sat on his chest. He tried shoving me off but I had him now. I kept digging him in the ribs.

"Okay, okay, your dad's not going back," he said.

"And?" I said.

"And I like your mom," he whimpered.

"What?" I said, letting him have my full weight.

"Aaaaaaargh. She's got a real job. She has the stall. And, and she has heaps of customers. And she's a great, great woman. And beautiful. With strong principles and high—"

I jumped off. That was good enough for me.

"Thanks, man," I said. "I didn't realize you felt that way. I'll let her know."

Paul was still rolling around on the floor clutching his chest and groaning.

"Ohhhhhhh. I think you've busted a rib."

"C'mon, get up. We've got work to do." I held out a hand and he grabbed it. I pulled him up then I climbed up to the loft myself, bringing out one of our older flying-bike prototypes. I passed it down to Paul.

"If we can get a bike in the air by Friday, I reckon New York's ours," I called down to him.

"Wipe 'no' and 'impossible' from your vocab. That's what your old man said."

"I didn't think you believed in things like that—little mottoes and stuff," I said. "I thought 'Impossible' was your middle name."

"Shut up. I want this thing to fly as much as you. I'm just a realist. But if we've got to get this up and running in three days, there's no time for reality. We've just got to go for it."

I wandered toward the back of the loft space.

"Remember the old MacPaul Flyer?" I called out.

"Yeah." Paul laughed.

We'd modeled our very first flying bike on the Wright brothers' *Flyer,* the first powered aircraft to land safely with a pilot. Or something like that. The problem was that the wings were gigantic and you pretty much needed to be at a major international airport to have enough space for take-off.

I climbed over bits of MacPaul Flyer wings and a never-miss basketball we'd been trying to develop. I shoved aside a rocket that we'd abandoned when we realized how much propulsion you needed to get something like that into space. We were only eight when we built it but we hoped to get back to it someday.

"Are you still up there?" Paul called.

"Yeah, hang on."

Right up at the back of the loft I saw another one of our prototypes.

"You want me to bring down the Flying Man?" I asked Paul.

"Ha! That thing was a joke," he said.

With the Flying Man, we'd tried to combat the big-wing problem by creating these little snap-out wings, Transformers or Buzz Lightyear–style. To make a long story short, they were total crap. They looked good. But I'd nearly died when I'd tried to fly off the roof of our bus and landed in the compost heap.

I scooped up some other bits of different inventions and climbed back down to the workshop.

"Why did we start building a flying bike?" I asked. "I can't even remember anymore."

"Flying transportation for kids," Paul said. "Something as easy and safe as riding a regular bike. Roads are dangerous and there's all that space up there not being used."

"A solo flying machine powered by renewable energy," I said. "That's what we always wanted. So what went wrong on Sunday?"

"Wind," said Paul. "The wing didn't deal with the wind."

"So how do we do it differently?"

"You need stability. Think about it. If you had three wheels rather than two, you could focus on getting the wing steady rather than steering the bike."

"Yeah, that's good. And the solar panels sucked," I added. "Too weak."

Paul pulled out the workbench stool and grabbed the sketch of Sunday's bike from a folder. I got busy on the bike frame, knocking out the dings and pulling the bent forks off. We worked side by side together till late into the night, like real inventors. Like men.

All I wanted in the world was to find enough cool stuff around town to survive in the competition till Friday. Then we'd have our shot at getting the bike into the air in front of hundreds of thousands, maybe millions of people. That was the dream.

Wednesday

6:12 a.m. I was up early and conned Mr. Kim into firing up one of the Web computers. He wasn't too happy about it but I'd been thinking about something all night and I had to check it. I knew the results from yesterday wouldn't be online till eight so I googled "cool." When I had thought about it in the night, I'd realized I wasn't even sure what the word meant. I found a bunch of Wiki entries and dictionary defs but I found this answer in a chatroom and I liked it best:

> **"It means doing your own thing and not conforming just to make other people happy. Work out your own opinions, respect people, and follow your own thing. Otherwise you're not human. You're a photocopy."**

I took a look around to see if Mr. Kim was about to boot me off but he was out in the kitchen chopping stuff up. So I cracked open my blog and just started freewriting on "cool." Here's what I wrote:

what is cool?

ive never even thought about what cool is before. i mean why would i? cool's just . . . cool. like hot but different. less intense than hot. but definitely not cold. maybe it's something to do with music? but what kind of music? and is cool sporty or not sporty? my mom told me that salvador dali, this artist with a weird mustache, reckoned the next big thing in fashion was whatever was out of fashion now. so maybe he thought uncool was cool. so does that mean my dad's cool? because he's so not-cool. but then his lightning farm is cool. so is it only certain uncool things that are cool?

maybe cool is on the inside. but then cat seems to think cool is all about outside stuff.

a list of stuff i think is cool:
movies, flying, creating, inventing, new york city, hokkien noodles, yellow cabs, things that move fast, adrenaline, dreaming, doing your own thing, writing my blog, jewels i spose in a kind of uncool way, the beach, cat . . . but is cat really cool? why? she thinks im a loser. ive got to try 2 not like her but i cant stop thinking about her. im an idiot.

cat if you're somehow reading my blog im only kidding about liking you. you're actually a freak.

i just surfed around n found this thing on flow on the web. this is what cool really is . . . flow is when you're so into something that you forget about time. you love it so much that time just disappears. everything else disappears. like when i'm creating stuff or working on a new idea or flying. FLOW is my idea of cool.

till whenever.
mac.

⊣ Coolhunting ⊢

8:13 a.m. Paul and I had been out for ages scoping the streets of Kings. For a town that was supposed to be one of the hottest places on earth right now, it sure seemed cool-starved from where we were standing. Yeah, there were whales cruising by, dolphins and the shipwreck at Samsara, surfers out at Blowing Rock—but we were looking for something explosive and different from anywhere else, something we thought was the greatest thing we'd ever seen. I knew that I'd know something was cool when I saw it but I just wasn't feeling the vibes.

We'd filmed a chubby couple eating chocolate croissants and making out on the rocks at Little Cove, a street-cleaner picking up tourists' wrappers and junk, a Doberman sniffing a Labradoodle's butt in the park, a woman in Lycra stinking of perfume charging up the beach—barking something about real estate into her cell phone, two backpackers with drool hanging from their mouths sleeping on the beach, a bunch of drowned sewer rats having a surfing lesson, and rich folks jamming their faces with nineteen-dollar waffles at a café. Clearly all the cool people were still in bed.

"Let's go check the results," I said to Paul as we crossed Beach Road toward the sand. The beach was the fastest way to school on foot.

That's when we saw Cat. Camera in hand, she was hanging on the corner near the Beach Café—black jeans and T-shirt, black spiral speared through her left ear, silver lip ring, black-and-white checked Converse sneaks. She was about the coolest thing we'd seen all morning.

"Can I shoot her?" I asked Paul.

"Be my guest," he said.

"With the camera," I said.

"No, let's go. It's after eight. I don't want to hear the result from her unless it's a win," Paul said.

We turned to cross Beach Road again when we heard the dreaded cry: "*Bonjour*, losers."

We stopped, turned, and Cat was standing there, holding something out to us. A piece of paper.

Paul tried to stop me but I walked over to her.

"Have you seen the latest?" she asked, straight-faced.

I held her gaze for a few seconds, then I snatched the paper. I didn't want to look. But I had to. Paul scowled at Cat and peered over my shoulder.

Our vid had 21,422 votes! But Cat's fashion thing had

39,746. We'd made up a ton of ground from Monday's results but we'd still been slaughtered.

Cat said, "I really feel for you guys. I mean, that's totally sweet, you thinking that lightning is cool, but I really don't think you quite 'get' coolhunting."

I scanned the sheet for the comments:

is this guy kidding? lightning farming is insane. no one knows where or when lightning is going to strike, so how do you get a reliable source?
– GeekSpace9, Mt. Victoria, Australia

I disagree. It could be a viable alternative energy. Check out the farm at www.mobilelightningfarm.com.
– Tad Cunningham, Little Rock, Arkansas, U.S.A.

How hot does cat look in her vlog?
– RockRollHarlen, Tromsø, Norway

This is crackpot science from the lunatic fringe.
– TasminDarko, Pretoria, South Africa

i go 2 mac slaters skool n someone told me tha crazy lightning guy is his dad and hes done time. anyone know what for?
– Chingy736, Kings Bay

Cat interrupted with: "Did I tell you? I'm having a party Friday night. A little *bon voyage* before I head off to NYC. Filthy Lemonade is playing. You guys can watch it on the Web." She smiled and walked off.

"Cow," said Paul.

"But did you see her teeth? They're, like, perfect," I said.

"Stop," Paul snapped at me. "She hates us. If she wasn't crushing us in this competition, she'd have Egghead kill us. She is not a nice person."

I watched her walk away. "Yeah, but 'nice' isn't everything," I said.

Paul slapped me on the back of the head.

"I'm kidding. Sorry."

"And Filthy Lemonade?" Paul said. "What the hell is that?"

"I dunno, aren't they on KROQ and stuff?" I asked.

"Great. I'm depressed. We gotta get to school," Paul said. We took the beach route and Paul moaned the whole way about how it was all over for us. I pretended that it wasn't, even though we'd scoured the whole town and it was a cool-free zone.

About halfway there, I saw a rainbow-colored kite in

the sky up ahead. Next minute we saw Jewels running toward us—purple headband, school uniform, purple Doc Martens—breathless.

"I've been looking for you everywhere. There's something you've got to see."

I was kind of surprised she was so friendly after she'd walked off from me at lunch the day before.

"What is it?" Paul asked, flicking his hair back, trying to look fresh for Jewels.

"Come see. You'll love it."

She grabbed my hand and dragged me. Paul looked a little jealous and followed close behind.

"I hope he's still there. This is so you guys. You have to film it for your thing."

As we closed in, I saw what was going down. The kite, almost the size of our bike wing, was attached to a guy with a harness. He had a handle out front to control the kite, then he had a skateboard strapped to his feet, carving up the beach. And it wasn't just any old skateboard. This thing had super-chunky wheels and, judging by the amount of air he was getting, it was ultra-light.

He'd skate along the hard sand, work up some speed, then kick the board into the air and fly for three or four yards before landing it again. He even pulled off a somersault.

"This is hectic," Paul said.

"It's beans," I said.

"It's elephants and yow."

That meant it was good.

Me and Paul sat there in the dune and watched for ten minutes, jaws slack. Paul shot a bunch of it. I wanted to ride that thing so bad. Jewels tried to talk to us and I shushed her a couple of times. After a while I turned around to her and she was gone. I looked farther up the dune but she was nowhere. Then I stood and waved my hands, trying to flag the skate guy down. A minute later he saw me and skated over, ripping massive air and sliding to a stop in front of us, spitting a light coat of sand over our feet. The guy was about our age, maybe a year older. He had thick jet-black hair sprouting from his helmet, long shorts, odd socks. I hadn't seen him around before.

"Hey," he said.

"What is that thing?" I asked him.

"Kitesk8board," he said. "With an *8*." He carefully steered the kite down to the ground.

"I need to ride that," I said, moving in to touch the wheels.

"It's harder than it looks," he said.

"I'll work it out," I said.

"You ever handled a kite?" he asked.

"Yeah, we're working on a flying bike," I said.

"You're those guys? I saw what happened Sunday."

"Yeah, well, that was an accident. Bit of bad luck. Can I have a ride?"

"No way," he said. "I built this thing myself. I can't afford anything to happen to it."

"I'll pay for it if I bust it," I said, not knowing how I'd do that, but knowing that I needed to ride that board.

He looked at me for a long time, then at Paul.

"I don't think so, buddy."

He unstrapped his feet from the board, grabbed it, and started moving off toward the kite, which was blowing around on the sand. I followed him.

"We're hoping to get our bike up again in the next couple of days and it'd really help if I could have a ride," I said.

"I saw how badly you wiped out. Sorry, man."

"Well, can we at least shoot some more footage of you? I'm a coolhunter." That was the first time I'd said it and it felt good. I guess I was a coolhunter now. I finally felt like I was on a proper coolhunt. Kids were gonna eat kitesk8boarding up.

"What's a coolhunter?" he asked.

I went on about coolhunting for a bit and, by the end, he was totally into being filmed.

"So, does that mean I can have a ride this afternoon?" I asked. "I live just up there in the Arts Village but maybe we could meet at Samsara?"

He grinned and shook his head. "You don't give up, do you?"

"Never," I said.

Sk8ing the Sky

Every time I leave earth behind for a second, even if it's only on a trampoline, I know that that is where I'm meant to be. I just forget about everything and feel the flow.

Three forty-five p.m. Samsara Beach. I started off with the kite, no board. Helmet and knee and elbow pads in place. I had to prove myself to Denson. That was kitesk8 guy's name—Denson Barker. Paul was behind the camera.

The wind was up but I still managed to keep the kite pretty steady. Being smaller than our wing, it couldn't lift you far into the sky but it was much easier to handle.

"Pretty good," he said after about fifteen minutes.

"Think I'm ready," I said.

"Whole lot tougher when you're skating," he said.

Denson rolled the board toward me and it banged into my ankle.

"If you break it I'll have to kill you," he said.

I looked up, smiling, but he wasn't smiling back. The kite

started soaring toward the ground. I panicked and just managed to straighten it before it hit dune.

Denson helped me slip my feet into the foot straps and buckled me in supertight.

Then he said, "I mean it. This is my life. Don't trash it."

I nodded, still confident but kind of scared now too. Denson was pretty built and he looked like he could actually do me some damage. And my anticrashing record wasn't that hot lately.

Paul bolted up the beach and got into position for filming. I took a deep breath and worked the kite into the air. I let it pull me along the sand, slowly at first, weaving side to side, getting a feel for the board. It had swivel wheels that you had to get used to. The kite swooped toward the ground and I pulled back with my right hand and it tore skyward again, pulling me along the beach as it did.

"Woooooooooooooooo!" I screamed. And then fell on my face and ate sand. Great. I was dead.

"Hey!" Denson called.

The kite dragged me along the beach as I scrambled to get back up. It pulled me along on my knees and then swept me up off the ground. It felt good to be up there but I was pulling hard on the kite handle, trying to get it under control.

Then *whooooom!* I landed and I was away, carving up the beach. The acceleration on that thing was hard-core. On the flat sand I was flying—on the ground, but flying. I was going way faster than I had on Sunday, and this was without an engine. It felt like I was sliding along the beach on the soles of my shoes, doing fifty. I had only about a hundred yards till I hit the Rock, an outcrop at the end of the beach, and I started to wonder if I'd be able to slow down in time. I pulled down on the kite handle but, rather than slow me, it heaved me off the ground and into the air. Just a little jump. But a jump.

I pulled on the handle again and I got about a yard of air and was up for a couple of seconds. The landing was pretty sketchy but the swivel wheels set me straight when I hit beach again. Now I was skating Regular rather than Goofy so I had to pull another jump to set things straight. This time I went up and spun around and the wind blew me nearer to the water. I landed in soggy sand and the wheels seized. I fell on my face again but the kite kept dragging me, legs scraping along behind.

By the time I stood upright, I was about forty yards from the Rock and still charging. A couple of little kids cut across my path, running toward the water.

"Hey, watch out!" I screamed, feeling a bit out of control.

The parents freaked and yelled but the kids didn't hear.

"Yo!" I yelled louder, but no reaction. Then the kids ran directly in front of me and I had the split-second choice to either go around or fly over. I pulled back on the kite, looking for air, but I stayed grounded. With two or three yards before impact I leaned back, turned hard, and dug into the beach,

...p a wall of sand and totally spraying the kids. I fell on ... and was dragged for a few yards before finally wrestling .. 1e kite to the ground.

Seconds later the parents arrived on the scene, sirens wailing.

"What're you doing, you cretin?" yelled the father.

"You could've killed them," said the mother, cuddling the two kids. I sat up and wiped sand from my eyes. The kids were maybe five and seven—a girl and a boy.

"Is that a skateboard?" said the girl.

"I don't care what it is," said the mother.

"A flying skateboard," said the boy.

"Watch where you're going," said the dad. "Those things oughtta be banned on the beach. There're kids everywhere."

They dragged their children back up to their towels.

"I want to go in the water," the boy cried.

"You can't. It's like Fifth Avenue down here," said the father.

"I want to fly," said the girl.

"Don't be silly. It's dangerous," said the mother.

Paul and Denson arrived, out of breath, Paul still filming on the run.

"How was that?" he screamed, pointing the camera in my face.

"Would've been better if I hadn't nearly killed the tourists. But, apart from that, it was insane."

Denson unstrapped my feet and turned the board over in his hands.

"No dings," he said. "You're lucky. Some of those moves were random."

Then he undid my harness and walked up the beach to the dune to check the kite over. We followed him up and took a seat on the sand.

Paul and I shot a quick piece with both of us on-screen, Paul holding the cam out in front of us. When we were done, he busted a Space Food Stick out of his pocket. He loved those things. I thought they were pretty wrong but I was so hungry I could've eaten a small dog.

"I'm going for a ride," said Denson after inspecting the kite.

"Mind if I film?" said Paul.

"Go for gold. I'll drop into the Arts Village someday," he said, "and pick up some footage. Let me know if you need a hand."

He gave me five and strapped on, slid down the dune, got the kite up, and tore back along the beach, somehow tacking into the wind and pulling some outrageous air.

"It's nice how light that thing is," I said. "Riding our bike is like trying to get a horse airborne."

"Yeah, and I like the beach start. No hill, no jump."

"Yeah, but we need to stay in the air for longer than the kitesk8board. It was cool but I wanted to hang there once I was up," I said.

"So we need something that's going to drive you forward in the air," said Paul.

We sat there for a minute thinking about it. A bunch of seagulls flew past, flapping hard against the wind.

"Flapping wings," I offered. Paul and I loved throwing ideas around like this. Our flying bike was suddenly getting its flow back.

A kitesurfer was carving it up at the other end of the beach. I started picking Space Food Stick out of my teeth.

"We should vlog Space Food Sticks," I said. "No one eats these things anymore and I'm kinda coming to like 'em. Do you think we'll ever go into space?" I asked. But Paul was looking up, thinking about something. A twin-engine, propeller-powered plane was buzzing out over the water. It looked like a seaplane.

"Maybe we need a propeller," Paul said.

"On the bike?"

"Maybe. Maybe on your back. Somewhere," he said, still watching the seaplane heading out over the lighthouse. "We can get into the air. And if we make the bike lighter, that should be even easier. It's just staying up that's a problem, so—"

"So we need something to propel me so that I can kind of drive through the air," I said.

"Yeah."

"That is an awesome idea," I said. "I'm so glad I came up

with it. Like you always say, I'm the brains of us. Or is it you that's—"

"It's me," said Paul.

"That's right."

"You're the guts," he said.

"The guts," I repeated.

"Stick to flying," he said.

"Flying," I said. "Let's go get this piece on the Web. If we lose today it's all over."

⊲ 'Dinner Rush ⊳

"Paul's mom gave me a call today."

My mom and I were in our tiny kitchen, at our foldout
table built for two. The light was warm. We could hear cicadas
chirping at us through the flimsy screen.

I was chucking back the food as fast as I could. It was eight
fifteen p.m. and Paul was out in the workshop building the
trike. His idea of a perfect meal was sausages without the skin
and egg whites, so he usually skipped dinner at my place. Raw
broccoli and zucchini didn't really juice his goose.

"Oh, no," I groaned through a mouthful. "How was that?"

"Fine. Sort of," Mom said. "But I can't keep avoiding her.
She wants to know what's happening with this coolfinding
thing."

"Hunting," I said.

"Hunting. She wants to have a meeting about it," she said.

"Oh, no."

"Don't 'oh, no' me. You're the ones not keeping her filled

in on what's happening. Or me," she said, looking at me. "So what is happening?"

I gulped a glass of water to wash a giant lump of uncooked rice down.

"It's no big conspiracy," I said.

"Mac," she said.

"Sorry, Ma, but it's not. We're just, I don't know, doin' this thing, and if we win we get to check cool stuff out. That's all."

"And what about the girl? Cat?" she said. "I wasn't sure about her energy. She seemed—"

"It's cool, Ma. I can handle it. I gotta go help Paul. We're tryin' to get the bike up again by Friday."

"Well, we have a meeting with Paul's mom tomorrow at Paul's place. Four o'clock!" she called as I slammed the bus door behind me. I tried to pretend I hadn't heard her. Mrs. Porter was my nemesis. She was everyone's nemesis.

I heard the door open again. "Tomorrow at four!" Mom called out.

"Got it," I said as I headed for the workshop, past the back-packers eating their cheap Wednesday night Thai.

My mom was such a worrier sometimes.

Propeller

Thursday morning. 7:02 a.m.

"Hello-o?" I called out.

Dad's dogs were going wild.

"Hello-o!" I called out again. "Dad?"

Paul and I were standing at the base of my dad's houseboat but the ladder wasn't down. It was about a three-yard climb up to the deck, and the slope of the hull was against us.

"Maybe he's out," Paul said.

"My dad never goes out. You saw how lumpy that milk was the other night. He drinks it even when it looks like cottage cheese just to avoid going to Safeway."

I looked behind us toward the big shed.

"Let's go have a look around," I said. "We don't have much time."

My dad's shed was an incredible place. If you couldn't find something there, it wasn't worth finding. It was the size of three basketball courts. One end was taken up by an electricity transformer and a bunch of other stuff for his lightning farm. The rest was rows and rows of shelves of pretty much any kind of junk you can imagine.

"You start at that end. I'll check down here. I swear he's still got it," I said.

Paul and I scanned aisle after aisle. There were fish tanks and old bikes, antennas and farming equipment, boat steering wheels, half an old car, bottle openers and samurai swords, a Super-8 movie projector, something that looked like the shell of an atom bomb, the carcasses of maybe fifty TVs, an aviary, two playground slides, and my dad's prized collection of forks.

After about fifteen minutes of searching I heard a call from the far end of my row.

"Here it is! I got it."

When I arrived, Paul was holding a propeller in a cage— an old paramotor that Dad had picked up at a garage sale and said that we'd fix up together one day. You used the prop for powered paragliding. You leaped off something high—with a wing but you also had a propeller to push you through the air. I'd pleaded with him to let me have it but he'd said it was way too dangerous. But that was when I was ten. Now I was pretty much a man.

"It's kind of broken," said Paul.

It was true. Half the propeller was hanging off and the cage was dark orange with rust.

"That's okay," I said. "We'll fix it. Let's go."

I helped Paul carry the prop through the shed and then kicked the door open. My dad was standing outside waiting for us. He was leaning against a fencepost, covered with grease, holding a wrench and some parts.

"What you got there?" he asked.

"Um," I said.

"That doesn't look like an 'um.' Looks like a paramotor," he said. "What you gonna use that for?"

"Well," I said, looking at Paul, who suddenly had bubbles of sweat above his top lip. "We're still trying to get the bike in the air."

"Mmmmm," he said.

"And . . . we tried to call out for you but you didn't hear and we just . . . I thought that maybe I was old enough to handle this now."

Dad took a few steps toward me and grabbed the prop. In daylight it looked even more useless.

"You want to fly with this?" he asked.

"Yeah?" I said, not so sure anymore.

He stood and looked at it, all its broken bits, for an uncomfortably long time.

"When?"

I looked at Paul again for some kind of reassurance. His face was almost white. "Tomorrow afternoon," I said, my voice cracking.

My dad peered at me through the wild mess of hair and beard that covered his head. He looked kind of like an angry yeti without the snow.

"Well, that's just stupid," he said.

"Thanks," I said.

"No, it is," he said. "I mean, if you want to kill yourself, go for it. It's all yours but I suggest you turn around, put it back in the shed, and get out of here."

I thought for a second about taking it but I was scared to tangle with Bigfoot, so Paul and I headed back inside.

"Your dad's awesome," Paul said.

"We should nominate him for some kind of award."

As Dad walked off toward the lightning field he yelled, "And bring back my wing."

Yeah, right, I thought. Saturday he'd have his wing back. Saturday when my life would take a whole different turn. If I was still alive, that is.

Paul and I dumped the prop where we'd found it, shut the shed, and tore off down Lighthouse Road. I hit the beach for half an hour's practice handling the wing before school. No trike, no board. Just me and the paragliding wing, a giant 'chute far above my head. The wind was blustery and it tore me around the sand a bit but my control was getting better. When big gusts came through, I managed to hold the wing steady. I practiced running in *S* shapes along the beach and nearly tore an arm out of its socket. No one said flying came easy. I skated along the sand on my heels, getting liftoff a couple of times. I can't tell you how good it feels—bare feet on sand, doing ten or twenty mph and hanging on for sweet life.

By five minutes to eight, Paul and I were sitting in front of a monitor in the library watching Cat's Wednesday vid.

Geeks or Revolutionaries?

Cat's vlog was on hemlines, saying that skirts were an inch shorter in Kings Bay this summer. "Groundbreaking research," Paul said. But she did model the skirts for the camera—which kind of tempted me to vote for her myself.

At eight Paul refreshed the page. As we waited the couple of seconds for it to load, I felt a big lump of fear in my throat.

"This is it," I said, knowing it could all be over. I tried not to care. The results pinged up on-screen. 32,384 for Cat. 33,182 for us.

We'd won by 798.

"Can you believe that?" I said to Paul as we sat there staring at the screen.

"Hardly a landslide victory," he said.

"Don't be a deadbeat. Is that all you can say? We're still in the game!" I said.

"Yeah, but—"

"Yeah, but nothin'. We are cooking, old man. We're totally gonna win this thing now."

Paul low-fived me and we read the user comments.

these dogs are gettin their geek on and im lovin it. I wanna kitesk8 cape may.
– Shadyboy, Cape May, USA

Who are these totally odd kids? I like the bloke with the big nose and the skinny arms.
– Sam, London, England

when does this kitesk8board start selling in france? i want two. and i want mac to teach me how to ride.
– JulieH, Aix-en-Provence, France

These guys are just rockin' it now. Cat's getting worse every day and these guys are howling along the beach doing a hundred!
– RockFish, Christchurch, NZ

This isn't even coolhunting. It's uncoolhunting. Like skateboards have never been invented? These geeks are trashing the whole perfection of the hunt.
– Cat DeVrees, Kings Bay

Geeks or Revolutionaries? I say Revolutionaries. Who says coolhunting has to be about products and makeup and how well you dress and haircuts? These guys are hunting Imagination, something you'll never know about, Kitty Litter.
– Paulo, Rio de Janeiro, Brazil

As we cruised to class for first period I felt like I was flying, like we'd actually gotten the bike in the air and I was coasting right over the top of everyone. It was 2–1 to Cat at the top of the second half. If we could win these next two days we were going to New York and I'd be a coolhunter. Me. Mac Slater. The kid without a computer or TV at home. The kid with a rat on the loose somewhere in his bus. The kid whose bedroom overlooks the chicken factory. The kid whose dad did time for standing up against nuclear.

"Hey, man, nice one," said a guy walking past in the hall.

"She's such a rabbit face. I'm glad you beat her," said a freckly seventh-grade girl.

"Yeah, I hope you guys crush her," said the guy walking with her.

I sat in class—math first up. My worst nightmare. Cat came to the door of the room and spent about five minutes hugging Rain.

Oprah, our teacher (dead ringer for Oprah Winfrey), got stuck behind them. "Excuse me, girls. Have you not heard the rule about hugging in the hallways? Break it up or you'll find yourselves in the principal's office."

The embrace came to an end and Cat skulked into the room, head down. Her cheeks were all red like she'd been crying. I felt a bit guilty. I didn't know she'd take the loss so hard.

Rather than sitting up front like she usually did (none of her group was in our class so the front was as far away from normal people as she could get), she walked down the aisle. She came directly toward me. I was sitting right in the middle of the room but suddenly I was all alone. I started to panic. Was she going to hit me or something? Maybe she was a black belt and she was going to kung fu my butt or beat me with a chair. What if she headbutted me or went for an eye gouge? Pulled off a special move and froze me? Imagine getting beaten up by a girl in front of the whole class. I seriously didn't need that.

What she did was much worse.

"Can I sit next to you?" she said.

It was like an old Western movie when the bad dude walks into the bar and the music shuts off and everyone stops talking and turns to him. The whole class was watching. I looked at the seat beside me where my bag sat.

"Wh . . . here?" I asked.

"Aaah, yeah," she said, like I was an idiot.

All eyes were on me.

"Yeah, well, I just, um, yeah. Let me just—"

"Quiet, everybody. Sit down please, Catherine," Oprah said to Cat.

I picked up my bag and my books tipped onto the floor. And my lunch. (Mom had packed celery with peanut butter inside, cabbage salad, and a raw carrot. It was like I was breeding rabbits in there. And everyone saw.) While I scrambled around under the table, Cat squeezed into the chair. I tried not to look at her legs.

"Okay, yesterday I left this equation on the board. Who thinks they can solve it?" Opie asked.

"Sorry," I said to Cat as I awkwardly crawled back up into my seat.

She smiled at me. "That was a good win," she said.

I looked into her face, checking for sarcasm. "You serious?" I whispered.

"Yeah. I totally respect winners."

"But what about what you said on the Web?"

"Mac!" Oprah called. "You seem to be talking to your new friend."

Everyone turned to us again and I went beet red.

"You must know the answer. Why don't you come up here and share it with the rest of us?"

"No, I—"

But Opie was holding out the whiteboard marker and she had that look in her eye. I got up from my chair and scuffled toward the board. Kelton Knightley stuck out his foot and

I tripped but stayed on my feet. A few girls laughed. Oprah was working on the board and didn't see it. I wanted to rip his nose off but I kept my cool. I didn't need any more attention this morning. I made it to the board and she gave me the marker.

"Um . . ." I said. There were figures on the board that I'd never even seen before. Were they Egyptian, maybe? Paul was our numbers guy. I was on words and action.

"If you are going to be a pilot, Mac, you had better learn how to count. Any other geniuses in the room?"

Pretty much the whole class stuck up their hands as I slunk back to my seat.

"Cat?" said Oprah.

Cat pushed back her chair and brushed past me in the aisle, supercasual. With a few swift strokes, she jotted an answer and dropped the marker on the rack under the board.

"Good," said Oprah. "At least someone has been paying attention. Perhaps you can assist your friend there."

Cat sat down next to me. "Don't worry," she said. "Like we're ever going to use this stuff." That made me feel a little better. I tried to concentrate on the class but it was like I was wearing earmuffs. Cat DeVrees was my entire world. My eyeballs were kind of hurting from peering at her out of the side of my sockets.

"Anyway," she whispered once Opie had sat down and left us to chew on a bunch of numbers. "I just wanted to say that you and I are cool. It's good you won. That beach-skateboard-kite thingy looked divine against the sunset."

"Yeah, I wish we'd invented it."

"You guys invent quite a bit of stuff, right?" she said.

"Yeah."

"Where do you do it? Do you have, like, a garage or something?"

"A workshop. Over at the Arts Village," I said. It felt good to be chatting to her. She had this really smooth sound to her voice, and she spoke well.

She stopped working and looked at me.

I looked up from my book.

"What do you say we try being civil to one another?" she said. She always used words like "divine" and "civil."

"Really? Didn't you totally dis us on the website?"

"I was just a bit annoyed that I'd lost," she said. "But I'm absolutely fine now. What do you think? Friends?"

"Really?" I said.

"Yeah. Really," she said, pinching my cheek. "You're incredibly cute. You can't believe it, can you? 'Oh my God, THE Cat DeVrees wants to be my friend.' I guess it is pretty amazing for you. I mean it's not like I knew you were even alive until now. But that doesn't mean we can't become friends."

I wasn't quite sure what to say. *THE Cat DeVrees?* Was she serious, calling herself that?

"I guess not," I said, wondering if this was a dream and thinking that the pinch on the cheek probably would have woken me if it was.

Cat and I didn't chat much after that but she helped me with some problems.

The bell rang. She gathered her things in one move. "Catch you later," she said. "And tell Pete we're cool too."

"Pete?"

"Your friend," she said.

"Paul," I said.

"Yeah, whatever," she said. "Tell him hi from me."

And I watched her go. "See ya, Cat," I said.

She disappeared into the hall.

I couldn't believe it. I chucked my books into my bag and scurried for the door. In the crush of kids outside, I managed to find Paul on the way to English.

"What do you reckon?" I said after giving him a blow-by-blow account. We walked into the room and grabbed a seat. Mrs. Astin was copying a quote from *Othello* on the board. Shakespeare was kind of my enemy right now. Up there with Paul's mom. We weren't even s'posed to be studying it yet but Astin was obsessed.

"It's a joke," Paul said.

"She really wants to be friends."

"You're so gullible," he said, spilling his books out of his bag.

"I'm not. She's for real," I said, sounding almost pitiful.

"You're pathetic," he said. "Think about it. Why would she suddenly want to be friends with you?"

I had to think for a second. "She respects guys that win. And we were losers before. Don't you see? We're in her league now. We just had to prove ourselves."

Paul shook his head. "Love does weird things to people's heads."

"As if I love her. I just think she's—"

"Hot," he said. "I know. It's disgusting. Are you gonna spend your life falling for every girl who doesn't look like my grandma?"

"Man, if you'd been there," I said. "We were, like, equals. She even said it—that you and I didn't exist for her till now. I feel so good, like this weight's been lifted. Maybe this is what people mean when they say they've been 'born again'?"

"That's a Christian thing, freak. My aunt Bunnie's one of them. If you're gonna believe her, don't talk to me," Paul said, and he grabbed his things and moved across the aisle.

"Cat said to say hi," I said as a last-ditch attempt to sway him.

He turned and gave me black eyes of death that threatened to spit blood at me if I didn't shut up.

So I did. I started copying the quote. Even if Paul was right—which he wasn't—but even if he was, it felt good to be included by someone like Cat. I'd spent my whole life feeling not exactly like a loser but kind of loser-ish, y'know. Different.

Like I'd never be accepted by certain people because I was from a weird family or something. I mean, I didn't see a movie till I was eight. I didn't use a computer till I was ten. Mine was not a normal childhood. But now that was kind of changing. "Geek chic," some dude had called it on the Web. "Gettin' your geek on." Whatever it was that we were doing, Cat was liking it. And that felt good. It really did.

Mrs. Porter

"First of all, I want to know who gave you two permission to do something as dangerous as trying to fly a bicycle," Paul's mother said.

My mom shrank in her seat. We'd been sitting in Paul's living room for less than sixty seconds and the interrogation had already begun. His house was an orange-bricker in a housing development called Sunset Downs, built in the 1970s. It was deeply ugly and scarily neat. On the weekend at any given time there were at least fifty lawn mowers running on Paul's street, trimming any stray blade of grass that might have had five minutes to grow. Every house had tidy little garden beds that said to the world, "Everything's swell here." But everything was far from swell in the Porter household. Paul was the youngest of six kids, the only one left at home, and I swear his mom was trying to organize and clean him to death. His dad was a bank teller and had barely said a word since I'd known him.

I shifted in my seat and the plastic covering on the couch

crinkled in the silence. My leg was starting to stick. I remember the first time I strayed from the plastic-covered walkways in Paul's house. It was as if I'd taken a dump in the middle of the living room floor. His mom went gastro on me. She pulled out the vacuum cleaner and then bombed the floor with all these crazy chemicals. Then she banned me for, like, two weeks.

I was waiting for the day that Paul would come to school wrapped in plastic.

"Did you authorize this, Carolyn?" she asked my mom.

"Well, I don't know that I authorized—"

"But did you know about it?" Sue Porter asked again.

"Yes, I did, but—"

"Right. Thank you for being honest, Carolyn. Finally. Now, can you also tell me why Paul has been home late, very late, every night this week?"

"It's—," Paul began.

"No," said his mom. "I am asking Mac's mother. She may decide to give me a straight answer. But who knows? Why am I always the one kept in the dark?" Mrs. Porter looked my mom up and down, glaring at her long rainbow-colored floral dress and sandals.

"Well," said my mom, looking at me. "The boys have been taking part in a cool search."

"Hunt," I corrected.

"Hunt," Mom said. "And they, well, there were two ... Mac came to me and ..."

She was drowning. She knew too much. We needed a diversion. Like a turkey burning in the oven. Or Molly, their annoying little dog, going feral and gnawing Mrs. Porter's leg off. Or maybe the engine from a 747 dropping through the ceiling, narrowly missing us all but, sadly, crushing Mrs. Porter and Molly.

But none of this happened. So I thought I'd better step in.

"Mrs. Porter," I said. "We've been given the chance to, um, to take part in a competition and—"

"Who?" she said. "Who gave you the chance?"

"These dudes. Guys," I corrected. "Speed and Tony."

"Who?" she said. "Where are they from?"

My ma leaned forward in her seat. She wanted to hear this too. Paul stood and started sliding out of the room.

"Back!" snapped his mom. Paul reversed and sat again, avoiding eye contact with anyone.

"Well, they're from ... a website—"

"What do you mean, 'from a website'? They can't be from a website. Are they locals or are they from Mars? Where do they come from?" said Mrs. Porter.

"Well, they're from England. And France, I think. And they want us to be reporters, sort of. Well, me really but Paul's helping out."

"And what do they get out of it? You reporting for them?" she said. My mom's eyes narrowed. This was the big question. I thought for a second. And I didn't really know. I looked at the clock. It was nearly 4:20 and we hadn't shot anything for today's piece. I would have eaten a dog-food sandwich to be out shooting at that moment.

"Don't look at the time. You look me in the eye," Paul's mom said. Man, was she tough. You'd think she'd at least pretend to be nice in front of my mom. Wasn't that what adults did? I pitied the workers at the bank she managed. Including Paul's dad. I imagined her using the safe as a torture chamber for staff members who were twenty cents short at the end of the day. I cleared my throat.

"Um, well, I guess they get people visiting their site?" I said.

"And how do they make money out of that?" she said.

"I dunno. Advertising maybe?" I said.

"Right. And are you being paid for this?" she asked.

"Not yet but—"

"Not yet," she said, mimicking my voice. "Well, I'd like to meet these men. When can I meet them?"

"So would I, Mac," my mom said gently. "You don't know what you're getting caught up in. I mean, you may be sending out the message that all kids have to be cool. And I think what Sue is saying is that you may be assisting in selling unattainable lifestyles to—"

"No, I'm not saying that at all, Carolyn," said Paul's mom. "Please don't put words into my mouth. I think they're pedophiles."

"Not everyone on the Internet is a pedophile," I said.

"Well, let's arrange a meeting," she said. "And we'll see." Paul's mom was obsessed with meetings. "Where are they now?" she asked.

Sweat pricked my palms. I had no idea where they were. But then I remembered.

"The Great Barrier Reef," I said. "Maybe you could e-mail them?"

She forced a laugh. "Yes, well, oh, that's perfect, isn't it? I'm sure they'll be very nice on e-mail. That's the way to find out if they're criminals or not."

How did she manage to make this whole thing sound wrong?

I looked to Paul. He was squeezing a zit. He did that when he was nervous.

"Look, I don't particularly care what Mac's mother is going to do but, Paul, you're not to have any further part of this until I have met with these men and found out exactly what it is they are after. And Carolyn, I'd appreciate it if you could be on my side on this one and ensure that the boys aren't sneaking around."

"Well, I don't think they've—"

"Thank you," said Paul's mom. "Now, if you don't mind

I have to get back to the bank for lockup. Some of us have jobs."

She ushered us out of our seats, straightened the couch plastic, and showed us the door.

It was just the start of a very bad afternoon.

Intruder

The workshop door hung wide open.

It wasn't exactly a high-security facility but, around here, it didn't need to be. At least I didn't think so. But someone had snapped the green bike chain we used to secure the doors.

"Hello?"

No response.

"Anybody there?" I said again. The workshop was dark, sheltered from the afternoon sun by the mangrove trees. It was quiet, too. I picked up a stick and ventured closer to the door, pressing myself against the outside. I breathed for a second, wondering who would bother to break into our workshop.

"Hey!" I called sharply, trying to catch them off guard, as I swung into the mouth of the doorway.

No one. I slowly moved inside, stick pointed. I wasn't too sure how a twig was going to stop a ruthless thief but it was the best I could do at short notice. I scanned the room. Our half-assembled trike was still there. We'd been planning to vlog a test run with the trike for today's entry.

I checked that none of our tools were missing. Then a bolt of panic jarred my body. I dived up the ladder and checked under the old painting drop cloths where we'd hidden the camera in its box late the night before.

"No way," I whispered as I pulled the sheet away.

The box was there. But the camera was gone.

Whoever had broken in knew what they were looking for. I checked my watch. Five on the nose. I had three hours to get my Thursday vlog up and stay in the competition. I had no camera, no camera guy, and a poorly assembled trike.

I thought back to Cat asking me in math that day where our workshop was. But I pushed the thought away. She wouldn't do that. I mean, we were friends now.

2 Hours and 46 Minutes to Go

"Psssst," I hissed.

No reaction.

"Pssssssssssssst."

Nothing. Did this guy have ears?

Paul was sitting on his bed, his back to the open window. I was standing on the Porters' incredibly clean garbage can in the pathway beside his house, down by the hot-water heater. I was praying that Molly, the little rat, wasn't snorting around in the backyard, ready to blow my cover. Mrs. Porter's car was back, and I imagined she wouldn't be too keen on seeing me so soon.

"Paul!" I whispered.

Nothing.

I grabbed the Hacky Sack from my pocket and threw it at him. He finally turned around, annoyed. He'd been counting his bread-tie collection again. Paul collected those little plastic things that go around the neck of the bread. He'd always start counting and get distracted halfway through and lose count. He reckoned he had about ten thousand but I thought it was closer to two thousand. He got excited about rare colors, like a purple one he'd gotten when he was on vacation in Oregon.

"What?" he said. "Whaddya want? I lost count, you idiot!"

"Sorry. I just thought I should let you know the camera's gone," I said.

"What?" Paul scrambled across his bed to the window and about a thousand bread ties scattered to the floor. "Gone? Where? Why? How do you know?"

I told him the story.

"You gotta come," I said. "We've got to get the trike together somehow and have a crack at getting it up. I don't have anything else to vlog."

He looked at me like I was insane.

"You're insane," he said. "Aircraft cannot be assembled in an hour. I don't know where we can get another camera, and Mom's gonna kill me if I go with you."

"And?" I said.

He exhaled loudly. "Just give me a second. I'll grab my shoes."

I smiled and, at that very moment, the lid of the garbage can collapsed under my weight. I fell halfway in with a crunch of plastic. Somewhere in the house the Rat started yapping and I heard, "Molly, shut up!" It was Paul's dad. That was one of the rare things you heard him say. That and, "I just want some peace and quiet!"

I tried to climb out of the can but my leg had been kind of wedged between the rim and the crushed lid. Paul stuck his head out the window.

"What are you doing?"

"Just hangin' out," I said. "I can't get enough of this can."

The Rat kept yapping and I heard the sliding door go at the back of the house. I kicked the lid in with my other foot, jumped clear of the can, and it fell over. I had no choice but to keep moving. Paul was trapped in the window of his room with no can to climb onto. He heard his mom coming around the back of the house. He jumped to the ground, rolled, hit the fence, and bolted up the path.

There was a hideous squawk of, "Paul Porter. Get your butt back here," as Paul and I jumped into the getaway vehicle—our bike with sidecar—and tore off up Sunrise Boulevard at top speed.

"She's gonna lose it so badly," Paul said once we'd turned onto Sunset Drive.

"Oh boo-hoo," I said. "Where do we get a camera, bread-tie boy?"

◁ Stakeout ▷

"Get your head in," I snapped at Paul. He ducked behind the enormous pine tree, one of about twenty along the beachfront.

We were across the road from the DeVrees house. Behind us was McMasters Beach, the most exclusive beach in Kings. I poked one eye out from behind the tree and gazed at Cat's place.

Imagine living in a house with no driver's seat, I thought. *Or smelling the ocean rather than "processed" chickens. Or having a bedroom without a "Push for Emergency Exit" sticker on the window.*

Cat's garage was at road level and there was a security gate on the right that led up some steps to her pool. If you followed the path up past the pool you reached the house—sandstone, three story, 180-degree ocean views, worth jillions. Cat's room was on the top floor, far right. Not that I'd hidden behind this tree before. I hadn't. Really.

"Just walk up there and ask her," Paul said.

"Why me? This is such a dumb idea."

"What else have you got?" he asked.

It was true. I had nothing. We'd already wasted half an hour at school, begging a janitor to let us borrow a camera. We'd tried the electrical store in town. Paul's old family cam had been trashed on Sunday when the bike had gone down. We'd even tried Denson but he didn't have a camera.

"You're going up there to ask her for our camera back," Paul said.

"There's no way," I said.

"You made out like you guys were practically getting married this morning. Surely she'll help her old buddy Mac find the camera that she accidentally picked up from our workshop."

"It so wasn't her," I said, diverting my eyes to the house. "She was superfriendly and she even said—"

The front door of the house opened and we ducked behind the tree again. Two girls came out. They stood there talking. I could tell it was Cat but I didn't know who she was talking to. A minute later they hugged, the girl headed down the path, and Cat went inside.

"Get down!" I said to Paul. "I swear you'd never make a detective."

"Whatever, Sherlock," he said.

"Who?"

"Never mind," he said. "Look!"

Exiting the security gate was someone we never expected to see. She looked both ways and seemed to stare right at us. Then she took off, looking behind her a couple more times, supersneaky. She crossed the road and walked along the beach toward town.

Paul and I stared hopelessly at the mess of bike parts sprawled around our workshop. Even if we'd had a camera, there was no way we were doing a test flight today. Or anytime soon.

We'd spent the whole ride back trying to come up with a good reason why Jewels had been coming out of Cat's place. We both knew there was only one answer. I tried not to point the finger but Paul wasn't messing around.

"She's the only one who could easily get in here without anyone noticing her," Paul kept on saying. "And we caught her red-handed on enemy turf."

"Yeah, but what's her motive?" I asked him.

"The most popular chick in our year wants to be her friend. She prob'ly flipped out like you did," Paul said. "Yes, Cat. Whatever you say, Cat. Can I lick your butt, Cat?"

"What, and I said that, did I?" I asked him.

"Yeah, you did. You wanna fight about it? Right here, right now," Paul said, putting up his dukes, old-school style.

"I'm not afraid to dance, dude," I said and faced off with him. We sparred, punches narrowly missing eyes, noses, and ears while we talked.

"D'you really think Jewels'd do that?" I said.

"I don't know why *any*one would believe Cat," he spat and landed a punch on my ribs. I pulled out a roundhouse and clipped him on the shoulder but it was all bone, and it hurt my knuckle more than it hurt him. "All I know," Paul continued, "is the camera's gone and I saw Jewels coming out of Cat's place on the day that Cat faked being friends with everyone. And Jewels can't stand Cat. She's worse than me. If that's not suspicious, then I'm heavyweight champion of the world. Now I'm bailing before my mom changes the locks." He started backing up toward the door.

"What?" I said.

Paul looked at his watch. "Open your ears, dipstick. It's nearly six forty. You're never going to get anything up by eight. Which means Cat wins. Which means we don't have to solve the case of the missing camera and we don't have to get the bike in the air tomorrow. Which means I'm going home. Bye."

He headed outside and grabbed the handlebars of our sidecar bike. It was standing next to the jump from Sunday.

"Stop, man."

He turned to me, shoving his glasses up his nose.

"I got an idea," I said.

He groaned.

"Give me till eight o'clock," I said.

"Give it up," Paul said and jumped on the bike.

"Eight," I said.

"Give—"

"You want to be back flippin' funky beefburgers for back-packers next week, or you want a shot at something better?" I asked him.

He stopped a few yards up the dirt path, hung his head, and let out a whine. "Your mom better be ready to adopt."

A Very Long Night

"What are you boys up to?" My ma was standing in the doorway of the workshop. It was dark outside behind her. Nearly nine p.m. and she'd just finished teaching a fire-twirling class. She looked tired.

Paul and I were attaching wheels. Denson was holding the trike steady. He'd dropped by an hour earlier to say he'd seen the kitesk8ing piece on the Coolhunters site and to see if we needed help. And we seriously needed help.

"Hey, Ma, this is Denson," I said.

"Hello, Denson."

"Hi."

"Paul, I don't mean to pry, but does your mom know you're here?" she asked.

"Um," he said.

I was impressed. I'd never heard them have such a long conversation.

"Hmmmm," she said. "Maybe you should head off home. Why're you working so late anyway?"

I didn't answer, pretending I was concentrating on wheel alignment.

"Mac?" she said.

I looked up. She knew right away.

"You didn't film something tonight after we met with Paul's mom, did you?"

I nodded. We had. It wasn't much but it was something. Enough to keep us alive till eight a.m. Friday when our fate would be decided. We'd been over to Jewels's place to confront her but her dad said she was sick in bed. Yeah, right. We knew she'd done it but I still had big trouble understanding why she'd sell us out like that.

So we recorded a voice-over on Paul's cell.

Then we nabbed the computer that has the scanner at Mr. Kim's and scanned a whole bunch of photos and sketches and stuff from our inventions over the years. We used stills of us swinging on the clothesline with dish towels around our necks when we were kids and me standing on top of the bus with my Flying Man snap-out wings, ready to make my headfirst leap into the compost heap. We showed a shot of Paul's house that he had on his phone, and we spent ten minutes using the phone to shoot footage of the Arts Village and our bus and even the chicken factory next door. We nabbed a Google

Earth image showing where in the world Kings Bay was. It was this whole mess of weird stuff that told people who we were. It showed how Paul was from a straight family and I was from a kinda loose one and how our inventions were like a crazy collision of those things—the patience to plan and engineer something (Paul) and the dream and guts to make it happen (me). It was rough and spur-of-the-moment and risky but there was something about it I liked. Anyway, it was all we had.

"Well . . . when does this trial end?" Mom said, walking through the doorway of our workshop, watching what we were doing.

"Saturday morning, eight a.m.," I said.

"If you win, let's sit down and talk about it. With these Cool people. And Paul's mom. And we'll see what they have to say. And if you have to travel, who would go with you and so on. Because I love you and I want you to make your own choices but I'm not packing you off to New York by yourself no matter what you say, okay?"

10:25 p.m. Denson had called it a night. Paul and I were working on the solar panels that we'd salvaged from Sunday's wreck. Kind of hard to test in the middle of the night. I couldn't believe I was going to be expected to trial this crappy invention in the morning.

"G'day," said a rich gravelly voice from the door.

I looked up. It was my dad.

"Your mother called me," he said. "Mentioned you could use a hand."

Mom and Dad hardly ever spoke.

"Yeah. But after this morning, I didn't think y–"

"Forget this morning. I'm here now," he said, kind of gruff, but probably not meaning to be.

The workshop light was starting to fade and it cast a weird glow on his face. He was dirty, like he'd been fixing a tractor or a generator or something. His feet were grubby and bare. He looked like he'd been roused from a winter's sleep. I knew it was a major event to get him down off the hill. I still hadn't spoken to him about prison and stuff. And I still felt a bit scared of him or something. Like going to jail must have changed him somehow.

"What have you got an engine on the thing for?" he asked, moving toward the trike.

"To get speed up for takeoff," I said.

"It's about air speed, not ground speed. If it's not going to propel you in the air, forget about it," he said.

"Yeah, but you said we'd kill ourselves with a prop."

"You will," he said. "You're better off just finding a big hill. No prop. You got any light in here?" he said, squinting toward the generator bike. "Still got that thing?" he said. Dad had helped us build the bike years ago. I was surprised he remembered.

I jumped on the bike and pedaled hard. The light started to

warm up. It was funny with my dad. Even though I didn't see him much, I always wanted to please him. Sometimes I'd think he didn't want to know me 'cause he never got in touch, and I'd get pretty angry, but then I'd see him again and all I'd want to do was make him happy. Even more than I did with my mom. It didn't make sense.

So Dad started working on the trike with us. He stripped the solar panels and engine off. He replaced some of the heavier trike parts with lighter ones from our abandoned bikes. He showed us how to attach the wing harness properly.

"Who's gonna fly it?" he asked.

"Me," I said.

"Tomorrow afternoon, you reckon?"

I nodded.

"We'd better do a test in the morning, then," he said. "You ever flown since we did it years ago?"

"Not exactly," I said. He knew that that meant no. "Do you think it's dangerous?"

"Statistically . . . Hold that and pull tight when I say," he said to Paul. Paul just looked at him. "You hear me?" Dad said. Then he lay down on the ground underneath the trike and bolted the harness into place. "Okay, pull." Paul pulled up hard.

"Statistically," he said again, standing and checking the top of the harness. "It's safer than riding a motorcycle and less safe than driving a car. We'll do some test runs. You'll be fine."

Paul stood and watched my dad work. He couldn't take

his eyes off him. Which was weird for a dude who said he had gerontophobia. Usually even the sight of someone over forty brought acid up from Paul's belly. But not tonight. He looked like a little kid watching Santa or something.

Just before the witchin' hour, the third parent of the night showed up at our workshop door. Paul's dad. He was wearing short stripy pyjamas and flip-flops. He had a bored, gray look on his face and didn't say anything. Neither did Paul.

"See you guys tomorrow," Paul said.

"Don't bank on it," said Paul's dad. He gave me and my old man a tired glare and left.

"Nice bloke," Dad said.

We spent the next couple of hours testing instruments and making final adjustments. We worked mostly in silence. I started to ask him a couple of times about prison but I chickened out. I was wrecked. Whenever I'd say something like, "I don't feel like I've seen you in ages," he'd say something like, "Can you pass me the Phillips-head?"

We finally quit just before two a.m., my eyelids stinging, too brain-dead to think straight.

The test flight was scheduled for first light—five thirty a.m. on the big hill down to McMasters. Do or die time.

FLOW

I was up over the trees. Gliding. Arms out. Everything super-green below. A mile away was the Pacific Ocean, stretching out forever.

I'd had flying dreams before but never this real. I flew over my school. Kids, teachers, cleaners were just specks bumping around in this mass of green dotted with buildings. It was like Google Earth in full-color, motion-picture reality.

I heard the bell ring but it was as if I was listening to it through a tunnel. Then all the specks moved on command and were sucked inside the buildings. I came to where Cat and her group were hugging one another and I hovered there, a hundred yards above. I didn't feel anything for her—love, hate, nothing. From up there, the most powerful kid in our year was just a dot like everybody else. Teachers and bullies, jocks and emos, the *A* groupers and the *Z* groupers, geeks and weight lifters were all the same. And nothing mattered to me—not Jewels or Paul's mom or their rat dog, Molly, or grease traps or who was cool or solar panels or living in a bus or New York or Dad or stolen cameras or Speed and Tony. From up there, there was no cool or uncool. There was just me and the air.

I wanted to feel like that all the time. Even when I'd landed and I was back down among it all, I wanted to feel like none of the things that usually bent me out of shape mattered.

I decided to get a closer look. I swooped down and in through the side doors near the art rooms. I cruised right over the top of the mess of heads below—kids swarming in every direction.

I was speeding right over them, a foot above their heads. I nearly smacked into James Campbell, a gigantic eleventh-grade basketball guy, but I managed to swerve at the last moment. The amazing thing was that no one could see me. I flew through the halls from one end of the school to the other. Past woodwork and English, math and social science, right up the ramp toward the biology labs. And even in there, surrounded by it all, I still felt good.

I shot past the office and out the front doors and was swept up into the sky. I was high above the trees again. I kept racing upward and, as I felt moist clouds touch my ears, I woke up. It was 5:05 a.m., Friday, the last day of the trial. The day of Cat's party. Mr. Kim was shuffling bins around outside. My head felt heavy and it seemed like I'd been dreaming that one dream all night long.

Test Flight,
◁ Friday Morning, ▷
5:58 a.m.

Helmet on. Top of McMasters Hill, right near Cat's place. Perfect wind conditions. Sun hot already. Butterflies in stomach.

We'd already aborted two takeoffs. One for crossed lines leading to my wing. Another for a car reversing out of its driveway and nearly wiping me out. I guess people don't expect to find three-wheeled flying machines tearing down the hill outside their place before six in the morning.

Paul had snuck out again. He was making last-minute tweaks. My dad? Nowhere to be seen. He meant well, but being in a certain place at a certain time just wasn't his gig. The sun was climbing and we had to go before the traffic got heavier or anyone from Cat's place saw what we were doing. She was only three doors up from where we'd be launching over the sand dune. We needed a spectacular spot for tonight's flight. The plan was to fly right over Cat's party. Maximum impact.

I took a deep breath and focused on the runway stretching

ahead—the long, steep hill down to the top of the dune at the northern end of McMasters. Once you hit the dune, the road curved around to the right and along the beachfront past Cat's place. But I was going straight ahead off the sandy slope. At the southern end of the beach there was a little cliff, and a screwup off there spelled almost certain death. The dune meant that if I couldn't get up, I had only a little way to fall to the soft sand that sloped gently down to the beach. Still, a million other things could go wrong.

I started to feel calm. I often got that feeling when one of our inventions was finally going to succeed. But I deleted the thought. I didn't want to jinx myself.

The trike felt good underneath me, a thousand times sturdier than a two-wheeler. I looked behind me. The wing was laid out on the road like a deflated parachute. It was being whipped around by the breeze blowing up the hill. Paul reckoned the air speed was about seven knots.

He patted the top of my helmet and I strapped it on.

"We'd better go before the lines tangle again," he said.

"Wish we had our camera to shoot this, just in case I'm not alive for tonight."

"Yeah," Paul said.

"You're not supposed to agree, idiot."

"Well, the fact is you could get toasted, man. Just like—"

"Yeah, I know. Like Icarus." Paul had wanted to call the trike Icarus after the mythological dude who flew too close to the sun with his wax and feather wings and got burned, falling to his death. I had talked him out of it.

"I'd better do this," I said.

"Break a leg."

"What do you mean, 'break a leg'?" I asked him.

"Isn't that what you say?"

"No, man. That's exactly *not* what you say."

"Just go," said Paul. "Before the wind dies or Cat busts us."

I squeezed the grips.

"Go or I'll kill you myself," Paul said.

So I let out the brake and started pedaling.

"Be scary!" Paul shouted.

I rolled forward and started to build speed. The wing filled with air. I pumped hard on the pedals. I had about forty yards before I hit grass in front of the dune and I needed lift by then. The wind in my face was good. McMasters often had an onshore breeze. Not great for surfing. Brilliant for us.

As I gained speed, I could feel the wing rise into the sky. I steadied it with my hands. The front wheel of the trike was locked and I was careering ahead without touching the handlebars. I just had to keep the wing steady. This is where I'd gone wrong on Sunday. No control over unexpected gusts.

I heard a weird *sssssssshhhp* sound in the wing above.

Then I felt it pulling me up. On Sunday I'd fought this lift until I'd hit the jump, but riding the kitesk8board and working with Dad had taught me that I didn't need a jump.

All I needed was enough air speed to give me lift.

A surfer sitting on his board beyond the breakers gave me a "Whoooooooooo!" and threw his fists in the air. I so wished we had a camera shooting this. With ten yards to run, I felt the wheels lift off the road and that familiar buzz all over my skin. The weird noise from the wing above was getting louder. I'd never heard anything like it and I took a quick glance up. It was superbright but I thought I could see a little rip in the wing on the right-hand side.

I had ten yards before I hit the edge of the dune and I was about a foot off the ground when I heard a tearing sound and I felt the right side of the wing collapse. I either had to risk it, fly out over the dune, and hope for the best, or ground the trike and see if I could stop before I hit the dune without wiping out badly. Either way was iffy.

Paul screamed something that sounded like "Stop!" so I grounded it on the edge of the road. Two wheels hit a rocky ditch, bounced, and I rose into the air again. I had three yards of grass before the top of the dune where the ground would drop away from me. I landed again, hit the soft sand. The wheels bogged down, the wing went flying forward, and then it tore me down the dune. I braced for the trike to flip. Somehow I managed to land the wing and then the trike tipped onto its two right-hand wheels, leaving me with a mouth, a nose, two eyes, and an ear full of sand. I stayed that way until Paul reached me a couple of minutes later, saying, "What happened?"

I wanted to scream at him and say, "A gigantic rip in the wing is what happened. Me almost dying is what happened," or something like that. But instead I said, "Can you help me up? Please."

All I knew was that I wasn't in the air. I was upside down on the sand. And if we couldn't get it up on a test run and we had a massive tear in the wing, there was no way we were gonna make our first flight at the party in about thirteen hours' time.

Assembly

"Please give our coolhunters a warm round of applause," said Mr. Debnam, our school principal. Cat walked confidently up the stairs and onto the stage. Paul and I had to squeeze past about fifty kids, then walk all the way down the center aisle from the back of the hall. I was kind of sore from the crash on the dune.

They'd sprung this on me in homeroom. Cat wanted to do some self-promotion in assembly so they had asked me to speak too. I don't know what she was thinking. Speaking in assembly was so the opposite of cool. She would never have done this before. I guess she was feeling the heat.

"Now, Catherine, can you please tell the students about your experience on this multimedia project," Debnam said.

"Yeah. Hi, everybody," she said, cute, with a smile. There were whistles and cheers from everywhere. "You liking my vlog?" More whistles and cheers. "You going to vote for me tonight?" More whistles.

Mr. Debnam leaned in to the mike. "Those ninth-grade boys whistling, you know what the policy is. Any more and I'll see you after assembly. Just get on with the report, please, Catherine."

Paul and I made it onto the stage and Cat grimaced at us like we were vomit. Things had not gone well for her overnight. She'd done her vlog video-diary style, head and shoulders, straight into camera, no other images, launching a vicious attack on me, saying, "I don't mean to be rude or anything but, seriously, do you want your 'cool' served up by a guy who lives in a bus? I mean, I went over and saw it with my own eyes and it's so gross in there. And I just wonder if Mac can honestly spend his time finding the coolest stuff on the planet when he's living, like, two miles below the poverty line. And the people around that Arts Village are scary. Like, they send shivers up my spine. All these people who totally don't wear deodorant and they, like, stink, and they all hug each other for, like, ten minutes. Not like *my* group does, but in a gross way. Seriously, you should think twice about choosing him. It's time to vote this backwater hippie off the island."

I'd been pretty devastated when I'd first seen Cat's Thursday night piece. But I was far from devastated when the result had flipped onto the screen at eight Friday morning. Tons of people on the site had revolted against her, giving us our biggest win ever. Subscribers totally dug the Arts Village and said the pic of Paul and me with dish towels around our necks when we were young was "cute." We got more than 50,000 votes and Cat had less than 20,000. The comments on her piece were way harsh too. Even Speed weighed into the debate, calling for calm. Cat was not happy.

"In terms of what happened with last night's vote," she said to the assembly, "which was totally unfair, but whatevs—I just want to say that I totally stand by what I did, showing this freak up for who he is."

Boos from the audience. Mr. Debnam moved from the side of the stage toward the mike. Cat spoke louder over the booing, "I believe you have to stand by what you think and just say it. Shut up, everyone, and listen! This is all a game and you do what you can to win. I'm not ashamed of—"

"Enough!" said Mr. Debnam. "Teachers, can you please identify those who were booing, Jacob Kennedy in particular, and I'll see them and you, Catherine, near the main doors. That is not the way we behave in assembly."

Cat scowled at him and slunk away from the stage.

"Now, Matt, if you can—"

"Mac," I said.

"Sorry?" he said.

"My name's Mac," I said.

"Right. Okay, Mac, if you can give us a very brief report and try not to make it an advertisement for yourself but, rather, give us some insight into what it has meant to be given this opportunity."

As I took the mike, there was a whole bunch of cheering. It was weird.

"Um, thanks," I said. "I just want to thank my man, Paul." I was more nervous than I had been before the test flight. There were a few whistles from the back and Paul went red. "We've kind of done this together. Um, yeah, look, it's been really good and, ah . . ." I was stammering like a football player giving an interview after the game. I had to pull something out of the bag.

"I just want to say that the thing that maybe I've learned this week is just that you never can tell. I never thought of myself as cool, I s'pose."

Muttering in the audience. Probably people saying, "Damn straight. You got that right."

"But then these guys gave me this chance and they saw something in me," I said. "And this week we've hunted some really cool people doing some really great stuff. Like all our inventions and the kitesk8board and my dad's lightning farm and—"

Cheers from the crowd.

"At the beginning we kind of had no chance of winning this thing, but it's come down to the wire and I just want to say that if there's something you're juiced on, whatever it is, if it's something where you're feelin' the flow and the rest of the world just disappears, give it a go and you never know."

Mr. Debnam took the mike.

"Thank you, Matt," he said.

I leaned into the mike again. "That's Mac. And if anyone's seen our camera, can you let me know?"

I scanned around for Jewels. Unbelievable. She was sitting up front with Cat and her followers. She wouldn't make eye contact with me.

"Be scary," I said into the mike, and Paul and I left the stage.

There were cheers from the audience. Tons of applause.

The bell rang and I headed for the door. My ma had written a letter to get me out of school right after assembly. Paul's mom wouldn't write him one but he'd try to bust out after lunch.

I had two small problems to solve—a bike that wouldn't fly and a missing camera to find. I had a hunch on who could help me find the camera.

"Hey! Jewels!"

I was at the top of the stairs that led from the lunchroom down to the main building, and I could see the back of her head in the middle of the crowd.

"Jewels!" I screamed again, louder this time, as I dodged down the stairs.

"'Scuse me. Coming through," I said.

"Watch out, pal," someone said.

I hit the bottom of the stairs and caught a glimpse of Jewels looking back at me from a window inside the building as she hurried off toward art. She looked so guilty. I ducked into the hall and pushed through the crowd, racing after her.

We had art together every Friday morning so I hung around till after class had started. But no Jewels.

Run

I broke into a jog, my breathing shallow, heart rate up. I knew they were after me from the second I left the building.

You know when someone's following you and they haven't even made a sound but you know that they're there? When I'd speed up, they'd speed up too. When I'd slow, they'd slow. And every step I took was taking me farther away from school and anyone who'd stop them from doing whatever it was they had planned.

I knew that one of the guys was Egg, Cat's boyfriend, the tenth-grade dude who had supposedly maimed a kid with a killer tackle at his last school. Another guy was Soren Berryman, Cat's cousin from eleventh grade, and I wasn't too sure who the other guy was. Together, they looked like the front row of a very ugly defensive line.

My feet pounded on hot tar that was partly melting. Another searing day. My bag beat against my back. I pulled the straps tight. My head thumped with the extra blood that had shot up there to deal with the panic. Not panic. I was trying to be cool. And I had reason to be:

1. I hadn't done anything wrong.

2. Maybe I could outrun them.

3. They probably weren't even after me. Maybe it was just in my head.

I didn't really believe any of this but I had to tell myself something to relax. I came to where the buses pulled in. I still had a couple of hundred yards of road running through forest before I hit the main road. There was a trail off to the left that not too many people knew about. It took you through some gnarly mangroves and spat you out on the beach up near the shops. I mulled over whether to duck in there and hope my knowledge of the trail would help me outrun them, or whether to just stay on the school road. But no cars were likely to come along at this time of day, so chances were that they'd catch me in the next hundred yards or so and who knew what they'd do?

I decided to go with the shortcut. I veered up onto the footpath near the mouth of the trail. I could hear three pairs of feet smacking against tarmac as they ran after me. I was trying to look casual. Just going for a jog, you know, keeping fit in the blistering heat of a day that was pushing mid-eighties already.

As I was passing the opening of the trail I made a sharp turn, and I was quickly swallowed up by thick, scrubby mangrove trees. Hopefully I was out of sight. I put the foot down and powered through, scratching my arms and legs up pretty bad as I ran into the darkness. I knew I had to get to the creek before they entered the trail if I was going to have a chance of losing them. My arms fired up and down like pistons and the ground was a blur beneath me. I wanted to look back but I couldn't afford to slow down. Sweat stung my eyes. I wiped at them with my forearm but it was thick with salty perspiration too.

I hit the top of a small hill that led down to the creek and I glanced over my shoulder, seeing flashes of color moving fast through bushes.

"Hey!" said one of them.

Damn. I powered down the slope. Rocks slipped out from under me. I was moving so fast I wasn't in control. My legs were tumbling down the slope, my feet working hard to keep a grip. The bottom of the trail near the creek was covered with tiny pebbles and I hit the brakes, trying to slow myself so that I could hop across the water. But as I slowed, my feet slipped and I fell, tearing skin off my legs and back.

It stung. I touched a leg and felt blood but, just then, Egg and the others came over the rise and started bolting down the hill toward me.

All I had to do was get over the creek and run three

hundred yards before the trail came out at the beach. I got up and hopped across one rock, then another, water streaming beneath me. Then I jumped onto a log and ran across it all the way to the other side of the creek.

When I hit the bank I decided to take a gamble. I stopped to shove the log away. Egg and the others were nearly at the creek edge. The log was heavy but I got some movement. With another shove, it started to drift away and I gave it a kick, leaving an impossible jump between the last rock, in the middle of the creek, and the bank that I was standing on.

As I turned and started racing off through the track I could hear them grunting as they jumped over the rocks. Then a splash and a scream from one of them. Then a whole bunch of splashing and swearing as the three of them made their way across the rushing creek.

I tried to power along the track but my legs were jelly with nerves and exhaustion. The guys were only about ten yards behind now. But they were big. My only hope was that size or ugliness would slow them down. I was an okay runner, had been to regional cross-country a couple of times, and I was light, so if I could—

Slap. Something heavy landed on my back and spun me around. Egg's hand. We were face-to-face, him breathing, panting, and towering over me.

"Why didn't you slow down when I yelled?" he said, out of breath and spraying spit on me as he spoke.

"I don't know," I said.

"We only wanted to talk," he said, face covered in tiny beads of sweat, eyebrows and ears bright pink.

"Right," I said.

"But that was before you made me run through the creek, you little turd," he said.

The guy I didn't know arrived. He was even bigger and uglier than Egg, with a head like a battering ram. Soren straggled up and doubled over, pinching his waist like he had a stitch.

"What're you gonna do about these wet shoes?" Soren said.

I looked down at his feet. What'd he expect? Was I carrying a blow-dryer? Did he want me to breathe on them? Piggyback him home to mommy?

"What're you laughing at?" he said.

"Nothing. Just . . . What do you want me to do?"

"Don't be smart," Soren said.

"Shut up, Sozza," said Egg. "Now, I'd like to mess you up right now but Cat asked me not to, so you can thank her for that—but make sure that whatever you have planned for tonight, don't submit it, okay? Even if you think you want to win and you want the glory and whatever, it's not worth it for you, all right?"

I looked him in the eye.

"All right?" he said, louder, tightening his grip on the back of my neck.

"Yeah. All right. No. I said yes," I said.

"Well, say it louder next time," he said, loosening his hold. I took the chance and slipped free, stepping back along the track.

"I'm serious," he said, the three of them shrinking away as I backed up the path.

"You hear me?" he said.

I didn't answer. I was about fifteen yards away, and I turned and broke into a jog, powering through to the beach. I didn't look back.

⊲ Crash-Landed ⊳

I could hear a high-speed whirring sound coming from our workshop. Through a window I caught a glimpse of a wild-haired man chugging on the pedals of our trike with his hands. The trike was upside down on the workbench. I unlocked the chain and pulled the door.

My dad looked up. "Why's my wing got holes in it?" he said.

"Why weren't you there and how'd you get into our workshop?" I fired back.

He glared at me. He wasn't used to me answering back.

"I was asleep," he said. "And I came in through the window."

He adjusted something with a wrench and then powered away on the pedals again.

"You weren't dragging the wing on the road, were you?" he called over the sound of the whirring. Then he looked at me again, knowing that we had been.

"We're only beginners," I said.

He scratched his head, trying not to get angry. But he let me have it anyway.

"Dragging a paraglider wing across tar? That is just the most ludicrous thing I ever heard." Then he went on and on, talking about how dumb we were. After a while I'd had enough.

"*You're* not exactly perfect!" I said.

"What's that supposed to mean?" he asked.

"Do you know how much hell I get at school every time you get arrested?"

"I stand up for what I believe in," he said.

"Yeah, I know, and you asked me not to contact you and you didn't tell me when you got out and you still haven't achieved anything by sitting in a cell for three weeks."

"Excuse me," he said.

"No, I won't," I said. I was fired up. "You haven't even spoken to me about what happened in the protest or what it was like getting locked up. You're my dad, right? I'm thirteen. You're the one I look at to see what I should be doing in this world and you won't even talk to me."

"Well . . ."

"You think you can tell me what to do and the way things should be done and you don't even know yourself. Do you know that there are people who stand up for what they believe but they don't go to jail or ignore their families? Why aren't you one of them?"

My dad was silent. I waited for him to get up and walk out. That's what he usually did. But he didn't. He just sat there looking out the dirty window toward the mangrove trees for what seemed like forever.

"I'm not a great talker," he said.

We were both quiet for a long time.

"I'll tell you about it one day," he said. "But when I'm ready. Not now, all right?"

He let out a breath and said, "Come here."

I stood, not really wanting to. I walked over to him. He handed me the wrench. "Hold that there and twist it when I say," he said. He chugged on the wheels again. "Now," he said. I twisted and he stopped pedaling.

"Tell me what happened this morning."

So I did. I told him the whole thing. The aborted takeoffs, the tangled lines, the cars reversing out, the smash on the dune.

"That explains why the frame's twisted," he said. "And the rear axle's slightly bent. When's your buddy getting here?"

"After lunch. When he gets out of school," I said. "Can you fix the wing?"

"We'll take it to a shop. You never fix a wing by yourself. Too dangerous."

"How much will it cost?" I asked him.

"Don't worry about that," he said. "Help me lift this off here, will you?"

Not a Great Night for Flying

By 2:36 p.m. a filthy storm was brewing. Major warnings. The worst we'd seen in ten years, they were saying. Hailstones the size of honeydews were already falling a couple of hours up the coast. Roofs peeled off houses like scabs off knees. The wind lifted three pigs from a sty and dumped them on a highway, causing a semi to smash. Pure evil in the sky and it was heading our way.

I pedaled the trike hard down Harper Lane and slipped down Styne. The feather that Mom had given me was taped to the handlebars. It was a seriously cool vehicle.

Paul was riding his skateboard and my dad was on his beat-up bike somewhere across town. We'd split up but we were all heading to the same place—top of McMasters Hill. We had to be low-key. A trike like ours was not something you saw every day on the street. We needed to get it safely to its hiding place before school was out and Cat discovered what was going down.

There were only two ways to get to McMasters. You could take the winding cliff road or you could ride along the sand from beach to beach, taking advantage of low tide and weaving through the rocks.

The cliff road was the only way for cars to get in or out of McMasters, and news of some weird dude on a three-wheeler with riggings for a wing would get around that little community pretty fast. It was the kind of toy that even the rich old dudes who lived at McMasters would cut off a limb to have a ride on.

So I decided to take the beach route. I had to move. The tide was coming in, and pretty soon the strip of beach around the headland would disappear.

I rolled down the lumpy concrete boat ramp near the Rock, my jaw juddering up and down. When I hit sand, I tried to power through but it was too soft. So I jumped off, picked up the trike, and made a beeline for the hard stuff.

Sand raged across the beach, pricking my legs like a thousand tiny needles. I still had my school uniform on. No time to change. Our plan was to get into Cat's party somehow and find our camera. If I made it inside, I seriously needed some new clothes. Speed might've thought school uniform was cool, but two hundred kids at a party on Friday night might think differently.

It was pretty scary knowing that we still didn't have the cam. Worst case, we could use Paul's phone again but it was pretty bad in low light. The party was due to kick off at five so that Cat could submit her vlog for eight and then party into the night. We planned to hit the sky at seven, in front of the entire party, just as the sun was going down.

The water at the point was thick with surfers. This always happened when a killer storm was coming. The waves were seven-footers and people were getting hammered.

I worked my way around the rocks on the sandy patches. At one stage I had to stop and climb over a treacherous stretch of jagged stuff but mostly it was smooth. I pedaled onto McMasters at 2:55 p.m., ducking in behind a clump of rocks at the bottom of my favorite sand dune. The surf was still massive at McMasters but the wind wasn't so bad. In fact, it seemed almost too still.

I peered over the rocks. Cat's place was a hundred yards up the beach. I could see someone outside, either cleaning the pool or setting up for the party. Was Cat already home? Maybe she'd gotten off early too. I imagined myself soaring over the party, the looks on everyone's faces.

I couldn't see if Dad and Paul were at the meeting place at the top of the hill yet. Sometimes it really didn't pay to have low-fi parents with a no-cell policy. What was the point of Paul having a phone if I didn't? The dude had no one to call.

Five to three. Time to make a break for the hill. There'd be kids everywhere in ten minutes' time. The person up at Cat's looked my way. I ducked, waited a few seconds, then checked again. They were walking back inside. I quickly wheeled the trike around the rocks, along the bottom of the sand dune, and up the stairs to the grass. Then I jumped on and pedaled up the road.

As I made it to the top, where McMasters met the cliff road, I heard a "Yo!"

Paul and Dad were over to my left behind a row of pandanus trees. I heard a deep mechanical groan and looked up to see the school bus coming around the corner. Disaster. I pushed hard and rolled the trike beyond the tree line, where Dad and Paul stood, just as the bus swept past. I spied Cat's head in the backseat but she didn't look my way.

We raced around finding palm fronds and other branches to cover the trike. If you looked hard you could still see something shiny underneath but it was good enough.

"What do you think?" I said to Dad, looking out over the water at the storm moving in.

He drew in a sharp breath. "Not a great night for flying."

Gate-Crasher

5:38 p.m. With lightning all around and the sky silvery gray, I wriggled my way under the fence. The bottom of the wooden palings tore at the grazes on my back, and I had the taste of dirt on my tongue. I was crawling into a garden. The rain hadn't hit yet but the wind was full-on, blowing the plants in every direction. There was a distant boom of thunder. Through the hedge and down the slope I could see the party was kicking off. The house was wide open, with big bifold doors, so you could see through to the pool out front, water blowing off it in sheets, and the ocean beyond. About fifty kids were on the dance floor by the pool where the band was setting up.

We were way up at the back of the house. We'd been circling Cat's ten-foot-high fence for twenty minutes before Paul noticed a bunch of rocks blocking a hole where a dog had been digging. We rolled the rocks away and, voilà! Our invite to the party of the year.

Crashing didn't feel so good. Not just because the row of

hedge bushes I was sliding into had about twelve hundred pounds of manure in it, but also because I didn't even want to go to the party. But we had to get our camera back. My dad was up the hill looking after the trike. Jewels was probably inside. She was the key to me getting the camera.

Once I was through, I waited for Paul's head to appear in the dog hole. But it didn't.

"What are you doing?" I yelled, trying to be heard over the noise of wind and music.

"Reereeroraa," was what I heard back.

"Speak up, moron. I can't hear you," I said.

"I can't do it," he yelled.

I crouched down and spoke through the hole I'd just crawled through, like I was talking to a bank teller, waiting for them to slide me my cash.

"You better be coming through!" I said.

"I can't, man. It's my claust—"

"Don't tell me that. I don't wanna hear it. Just. Get. Under. The. Fence."

As well as fearing old people and flying, Paul was petrified of small spaces. Squeezing through a hole under a fence into a manure-filled hedge really wasn't his idea of a great night out.

"You go. I'll find another way," he said.

I cupped my hands to my face. This was so typical. But I didn't have time to psychologize the dude into climbing under.

"Whatever, man. Just make it fast."

So, I was on my own. All I had to do was make contact with Jewels, get upstairs without being seen, search around, find our camera, and get out again. I was wearing my school shorts and a T-shirt from Target that Paul had brought me from home. They were now covered in dirt, dog hair, and manure. This'd be a piece of cake.

The Party of the Year

The second I stepped out of the bushes I heard a voice I recognized. The guy was standing in a wooden cabana with a hammock in it, yapping into a cell phone. He had a British accent.

I quickly backed into the hedge again as I heard: "Can you hold on for one second? Mac, is that you?"

Speed Cohen, one of the Coolhunters founders.

I shuffled farther back into the hedge, hoping he'd give up and think I was the gardener or some guy who thought the dress code for the party was "animal feces."

"Can I just . . . Can I call you back?" said Speed. "Okay, two minutes."

I could feel him moving in closer to the hedge, peering through dense foliage.

"Mac?" He pushed aside some branches and stared right at me. "What're you doin' in there, man? Come out. It's a party."

I figured I didn't have much choice.

"Hey, Speed, how're you doing? I didn't hear you calling the first time," I said, then felt like kicking myself for saying something so stupid. Speed shook hands with all that knuckle-slapping and skin-sliding stuff, like we were old college buddies. I didn't even bother trying to work it out this time. I wasn't in the mood. I looked like the biggest Loser from Loserville and I really didn't want to be speaking to him.

I edged out of the bushes, in full view of the party. I could see Cat milling around inside so I quickly turned my back. "Seriously, mate. Why are you—" Then it dawned on him. "Are you not invited?"

"Not exactly," I said, raising my voice over the sound of music, the constant groan of thunder, and the wind howling all around us.

"Right, well, we'd better give you a low profile," he said. "I don't wonder she hasn't invited you. I've loved what you've been doing, mate. Spot on, really. You take, like, totally uncool elements, like inventing, for God's sake, and make them cool. You're teaching us stuff that kids like. I mean, you're teaching kids stuff that they like and didn't know they liked. I even like your goofy mate. You just . . ."

I tuned out. All I needed was to steer clear of Cat, Egg, and his dudes and find my camera.

"You don't have a camera on you, do you?" I asked Speed. "No. Why?"

"No reason," I said. I didn't want to tell him I'd lost his

cam. I still hadn't broken it to him about the phone.

"You haven't lost yours, have you?" he asked.

"No. No way. Course not. I just . . . Paul has it. He's just setting up."

"What've you guys got planned?" he asked, grinning.

I felt the first chunky drops of rain splat on my head.

"Big secret," I said, thinking what an extra-big secret it'd be if we had nothing to shoot it on.

"Can't wait," Speed said.

"Sorry," I said. "But can we catch up later tonight? Is that okay?"

"Hey, sure, mate. No problemo. Storm's about to hit. You take care of yourself, okay?" he said.

"Yup," I said and took off along the back fence-line.

There was a strong gust of wind and the sound of a door smashing shut inside. A couple of kids started to close up the house. The rain was getting heavier.

"There's no way I'm flying in this," I muttered to myself as I ducked down the side of the house and snuck in through a laundry room door. A guy and a girl were sucking face in there, blocking the way through.

"'Scuse me," I said, squeezing past. They didn't come up for air.

The hallway on the other side of the laundry room was packed with kids sheltering from the wind. Guys dressed in Diesel T-shirts, girls looking like they'd stepped off a catwalk.

They must have had an ugly-ometer at the front door and banned anyone who looked nasty. Just as well I came in the back. I'd never seen so many perfect-looking people in my life. It was creepy.

On the wall in the hall there was an LCD screen logged on to the Coolhunters site. It was showing Cat's miniskirt vlog from Wednesday. To the left was the main living room, opening onto the poolside dance floor. To the right was a set of stairs leading to the floor above. I wanted to just go up, find the camera, and get the hell out, but that would be just as bad as someone breaking into our workshop. I needed to find Jewels. She had to help me.

As I walked up the hallway toward the living room, kids were staring at me. I heard a guy say, "Hey, it's that dude," and a girl said, "Is he even meant to be here?" She sounded kind of scared to see someone in a T-shirt that cost less than 250 bucks. It might also have had something to do with my new cow-dung aftershave.

In the open-plan living area that spilled onto the front and back decks, there were seven or eight LCD screens on the walls showing Cat's vlogs from the week gone by. In the center of the living room there was an ice sculpture of the Empire State Building. The wind howling through the big bifold doors was blowing drips of melted ice off the building.

Three guys finished closing most of the doors. Someone had towels down on the tiled floor, trying to mop up all the rain that had blown in. Outside it was too foggy to see the ocean. The trees around the pool were blowing violently. The band was dragging wet equipment inside—soaking amps, speakers, and drums. They did not look happy. Cat was there, holding a camera, and it looked like she was apologizing to them. Then she turned and headed across the dance floor, disappearing down the hall. This was so not turning out to be the party of the year. I scanned the room for Jewels but she was nowhere.

Then there was a loud crack. And another. And another. Something bounced off the concrete out near the pool. Hail. Giant lumps plunging from the sky. Within seconds the sound of falling hail was everywhere. A soaking Speed bolted in from out back. I wondered how Paul and my dad were doing out there. The whole party was silent. Even the music couldn't be heard now and nobody noticed me anymore. For the next few minutes everyone just gazed out the wide glass doors, watching this demented ice fest.

Pretty soon the area around the pool out front was white with hailstones the size of tomatoes. They were smashing the surface of the water, causing explosions, and turning the pool into this heaving, churning bucket of crazy.

I smelled food. Hunger fell on me like a brick. I hadn't eaten since before lunch. No one was watching so I wove my way over to the food table. I grabbed a plate and piled it high with bread and salad and pasta and shrimps. I knew I should be getting on with my mission and getting out of there, but the food looked too good. As I dug a giant spoon into the potato salad I glanced up and saw Jewels in an armchair over near the doors to the backyard. She was by herself, staring through the glass. She was wearing lots of makeup, a black expensive-looking dress, and high heels. I wondered whose clothes they were. I'd never seen her look like that before. She looked kind of great but superuncomfortable, too.

I made my way over and crouched next to her. When she saw me her eyes widened. She straightened in her chair and looked around to see if anyone was watching.

"What're you doing?" she asked.

"Eating," I said. "You?"

"You're not meant to be here."

"Neither are you."

"I was invited," she said.

"That's not what I meant."

"You'd better go," she said.

I looked at her. "Where's my camera?"

Her eyes filled with tears. No spillage, thank God.

"I don't know. Where'd you leave it?" she said.

I looked at her again.

The sound of glass smashing. A bunch of people roared at the front of the room and stepped back from the glass doors now being thumped by hail.

"I don't know where she put it," Jewels said. "I don't!"

I just stared at her. We went too far back, and she knew that

I knew that she had no choice but to help me.

"Stop looking at me, creep-o-zoid," she said and stood up. I stood with her, ditching my plate onto a coffee table.

"Go away."

"Please. Just tell me," I said. "What'd I do?"

She looked at me. "You don't know?"

I shrugged, feeling like maybe I should know.

"At lunch the other day, you treated me so badly," she said.

"You stole our camera because of that? Because I didn't want to talk to you and Imogen? Are you kidding me?" I asked. "Anyway, you showed us the kitesk8board thing the next day. I thought we were cool."

"And you snubbed me then, too!" she said. "Remember shushing me on the dune whenever I said anything?"

By the way she looked at me I kind of knew what was coming. It was the Jewels talk I'd been sidestepping since she'd kissed me on the cheek in first grade. I panicked and looked around. I wanted to ask someone for help but I was at the wrong party.

"I like you, Mac," she said.

Oh, no. This was it.

"I always have."

Please. Someone. Stop it now. I know she looks good and she's great and all that but it's Jewels! The girl my mom wants me to marry. The girl who can do no wrong. The girl I used to swim nude with in the ti-tree lake when I was three.

"Are you okay?" she asked. "You look sort of green. Do you need water?"

"No, I'm okay," I said. "Just, um, emotional, you know?"

Jewels punched me in the chest. "Don't be an idiot," she said. "This is exactly why I did what I did. Because you don't take me seriously. I feel like I'm some annoying little sister to you."

I didn't say anything for a bit. Then: "So you wanted to make me angry?"

"I wanted you to know I'm alive!" she said. "I saw you crouching behind your little tree outside Cat's."

"Really?"

"Yes, really. It's not just one thing, Mac. It's years of you walking through me like I'm invisible."

I looked away. I didn't really know what to say. Maybe I was turning into my dad—unable to string two words together when the heat's on.

"I'm sorry," I said, still turned away.

"What?" she asked.

I lifted my head, looked her in the eye. Man, she did look good. "I'm sorry for ignoring you."

She smiled. "Are you just saying this so I'll tell you where your camera is?"

"Kinda," I said.

She punched me again, but a little lighter this time. She looked at me for a few seconds. "I guess let's do it," she said.

"I've got nothing to lose. Hanging out with Cat and her Kittens is like a death sentence anyway. They're so self—"

Another glass door smashed and people scattered to get out of the way. Jewels grabbed my hand and led me through the crowd. As we were about to disappear down the hallway toward the stairs, I took a quick look over my shoulder. I wish I hadn't.

Cat's Crib

Above the crowd, I could see a familiar shaved head staring right at me. Egg. He tapped Soren, who was standing next to him, and they started making their way toward us. They followed Jewels and me down the hall, pushing kids aside. I looked into the laundry room where the couple was still sucking each other's faces off against the washing machine. It was as though they hadn't even heard the hail, the glass smashing, none of it. I thought about slipping past and out into the backyard, but the stones were still falling from the sky and I wasn't so hot on being knocked out. Jewels ducked under a rope across the bottom of the stairs and I followed her. We wound our way up into a second-floor hallway, then up another flight.

We could hear Egg and Soren behind us so Jewels led me down the hallway, ducking through the nearest door. I kept it open a crack, peering through until I saw them in the hall. I shut the door quietly and let out a long, steady breath.

Jewels tapped me on the shoulder. I turned, realizing that I was in a bedroom. Cat's bedroom. And she was in there too.

She was standing looking into a mirror in a connected bathroom at the far end of the huge room.

With all the insane cracking of hail on the roof, she hadn't heard us come in. I wanted to get out of there fast, before she saw us. Jewels did too. But I knew that there was a worse fate waiting outside. I could hear Soren and Egg talking. A nearby door slammed.

Jewels and I stood still, barely breathing. Cat was crying. Just looking at herself in the mirror, tears streaming in big black streaks down her face.

The bedroom was at the front of the house, looking toward the ocean. Every wall of the room was pasted with photos of models torn from magazines. Even the ceiling was covered. Thousands and thousands of catwalk pics of way-too-bony chicks sucking in their cheeks, Zoolander-style. But angry. Just like Cat. There was a walk-in closet next to the bathroom with racks and racks of clothes inside. There were dresses strewn all over Cat's bed and in twisted balls around the floor. There were shoes and bags too. And half-filled coffee mugs on a nearby dresser and all over the bedside tables.

The hail sounded like it was beginning to ease. That's when I heard her.

"My God, what the hell are you doing in here!" wailed Cat, sweeping across the room toward us. "Get out!"

I grappled with the door handle but I think I accidentally locked it and couldn't get it open. Cat stopped, like, two feet away from us.

"What are you doing in here?" she screamed. "And what stinks?"

I glanced down at my manurey T-shirt and school shorts.

"He wants his camera," said Jewels.

"As if I have it!" Cat said.

"Cat, he knows," Jewels told her.

"Whatevs. Like I'm going to give it back to him when my party's this disaster. What do I do, just let him win?"

I had a flash of the "other Cat" from math class.

"Why did you try to be friends with me?" I asked.

"So I could beat you!" she said. "You're so naive. It's like you're five years old."

The door handle started rattling. A heavy hand bashed on the door.

"Cat? You in there?" Egg's deep voice asked.

I waited for Cat to open the door and let them in so they could tear me apart.

"Give me a minute," she called, staring at me and Jewels.

"Why are you so angry?" I asked, keeping my voice low.

"Because everything sucks."

"No, not just right now," I said. "Always. You're always angry."

"Well, we don't all live in hippie heaven like you two. Some of us have lives. Some of us want to do something. I know that probably sounds weird for people like you who just want to sit around and burn incense and sing happy songs about love and draw on your sneakers and try to make your bike fly, but it's the truth of the world outside your little bubble. Neither of you will ever be a success because you don't want it bad enough. I've worked so hard to become successful and you've just been this total geek-freak-inventor idiot and somehow got lucky. I hate you."

She slapped me across the face. Hard. In that moment I kind of got over my obsession with Cat DeVrees. For the moment, anyway.

The sound of hail had almost died. Cat stepped toward the door, put her hand on the lock, and clicked it. Egg burst through. Jewels and I were behind the door. Through the crack, I could see Soren waiting outside.

"You okay?" Egg asked, putting his hand on Cat's shoulder. She was staring right at me.

I had one chance and one chance only to get out of that room.

The Great Escape

I grabbed Jewels's hand and ducked around from behind the door, slipping out between Soren and Egg.

We bolted down two flights of stairs and into the hallway. The music was off. The band was leaving. The hail had stopped. Everyone was filing out of the living room through the front doors and past the pool. There was broken glass, cracked tiles, and tree branches everywhere.

"You go," Jewels said. "They won't do anything to me. I'll go out the front with everybody else."

She kissed me on the cheek. The same cheek that Cat had slapped. Some other time I figured we needed to talk and find out what was going on. I heard Egg and Soren on the stairs. Jewels ran for the front of the house and I ducked out through the laundry room. The face-suckers were gone. I bolted up the embankment, through the yard, and toward the garden up back, slipping on ice and feeling the chill through my sneakers. It was still quite light outside as I disappeared into the hedge and made a dive for the dog hole. If I could make it through, I was safe. There was no way those two apes could get through a gap that small. I jammed my head into the hole and wriggled hard. I could hear Egg and Soren crashing through the bushes behind me. I knew that all they'd see were my legs and they'd pull me back through and snap me in half for gate-crashing the party, busting into the queen's room, and trying to win the competition.

I desperately dragged myself through, clawing at the grass on the other side of the fence. I pulled one leg under, then the other. Just as my foot was coming through the gap under the fence, someone grabbed it. I kicked and twisted but his grip was good. The hands started dragging me back. I turned my foot over and over again and managed to slip my shoe off. Then I pulled my leg through, scrambled to my feet, tripped, and rolled down the hill in the empty lot next to Cat's place. Then I stood again and bolted up toward where the trike was hidden. Home free.

But then I heard the guys behind me and looked back. They were climbing over the fence. Damn. I jumped up a sandstone retaining wall into the yard behind the vacant property and ran through the trees. A dog barked somewhere. The daylight was silvery and dim. I ran along the side of somebody's house, over a road, and through another yard, launching off a can to leap the back fence and landing with a crunch on the hail-covered ground in the lane. I bolted up the grassy lane till I hit the corner with the pandanus trees where we'd hidden the trike. Most of the branches had blown off and the bike was in full view. I checked it for hail damage then looked around. No Paul. No Dad. It was twenty to seven. Twenty minutes before the planned takeoff.

"Dad!" I said, as loud as I dared. "Paul!"

No answer. I listened for Egg and Soren. I could hear some distant voices. I looked out toward the ocean. Strangely, the conditions seemed pretty good for flying now but I didn't have a camera, a wing, or anyone to help me with takeoff. All I really wanted was to get through tonight without being pummeled. I thought about ditching the flight and just getting on the trike and riding off around the cliff road. But I knew that I needed to finish this. I wanted to do something that my dad had never managed to do—actually complete something.

I heard footsteps from the lane. My dad and Paul. Dad had the wing in a backpack.

"Where've you been?" I snapped at them.

"Under somebody's carport. We could've died out here," Paul said.

"Egg's coming," I said.

"Where?"

"They'll be here in a minute. We gotta get out of here."

Dad was attaching the wing to the bike.

"You think we can do it?" I asked Dad.

"Why not?" he said. "Wind's dropped off. Right direction. Conditions are good."

"We don't have a camera," I said.

"I can try shooting on my phone," Paul said. "Even if the light's too low to get a decent picture, let's just get this thing into the sky."

I looked down the hill at the chunks of hail all over the road. I looked up at the clouds, trying to remember some of the cloud stuff I'd learned on the Web. Lightning flashed on the horizon but it was a long way away. It was fifteen seconds before we heard the tiniest rumble.

I knew I was going to do it.

I stayed on watch for Egg and Soren while my dad and Paul rigged the harness and wing. It was like Paul had totally forgotten that Dad was old. They were working together like cogs in a clock.

By the time I was sitting in the trike, helmet on, ready to rock, a few kids from the party had gathered around, wondering what we were doing.

"Can you help me out?" Paul asked them.

A couple said yeah.

"Good." Paul gave me five, whacked me on the shoulder, and said, "Be scary, man. We're never gonna have a better excuse than this to get into the air. You do this, we could be made men in this town."

I laughed.

"I'm serious, man. Made men in New York, even," he said.

He headed off, then he turned and said, "But I kind of want you to live too. So don't die, okay?"

He went down the hill with his group, clearing branches from the strip. Rather than ride on the road and trash the wing again, I was going to shoot down the flat grassy stretch on the left-hand side, which ended at the top of the dune.

Out over the ocean spears of sunlight shot through the clouds onto the water. Then they disappeared again.

"Hey!" I heard a call from my right. Egg and Soren were running toward me from the far end of the lane. "You're gone," Egg yelled.

"Yep, you're right. Go," Dad said.

And I was. Gone, that is. The wheels crunched over hail. Egg and Soren ran out of the lane and across the road toward me, so I floored it, pedaling hard. But they were still gaining on me and I had a wing dragging behind, sliding along the grass.

I felt a tug. Egg had grabbed a handful of kite strings. I pedaled hard but he was slowing me. I had a flash in my head of him ripping me out of the trike and onto the grass and turning me into Cat food.

⊲ Coolhunting ⊳ the Sky

A gust of wind shot up from the beach and tore the wing into the air, probably cutting Egg's fingers up pretty bad and nearly launching him. I pedaled hard, charging down the strip, leaving Egg sprawled on the grass behind. With twenty yards to go the wing snapped into the overhead position. Suddenly I was steaming toward the dune, wing up, Egg and the other idiot left in the dust.

Down near the bottom Paul and his group were holding kids back so they wouldn't walk across my path. A whole crowd was looking on. Up near the rocks at the southern end of the beach I could see a flame spinning around. She'd said she'd be here. I glanced at the feather taped to my handlebars and sent out a prayer.

With fifteen yards to go I felt a little lift from the wing and that thrill in my stomach shooting all the way out to my fingers. I bounced once and then I was cruising about a yard above ground level. I worked with the wing and kept it steady overhead as I soared toward the edge of the dune. When I hit the edge, I half expected to drop out of the sky again and face-plant.

But I didn't. I felt another big lift and I shot into the air quite quickly. It was something my dad called ridge lift—air that hits a steep surface and shoots upward, filling your wing and taking you with it. I looked down below and I was about twenty yards over the dune.

There were cheers from back on the road. I let out a laugh. It was incredible. This was the highest I'd ever been. By the time the bottom of the dune met flat sand, I was about fifty yards over the beach. I flew out toward the southern end where my mom was twirling fire. I thought I'd be supernervous when this moment came but I wasn't. The wing felt steady. Every movement of my hands shifted my direction and adjusted the wing. I felt in control. As I soared over my ma she looked up and watched me cruise by. I felt like I could almost feel the heat of the flames.

Now I had to turn. I could either head out over the water or make a fast turn before the cliff face and come back over the beach. I figured trying my luck with sharks probably wasn't the best plan on my maiden voyage so I banked hard, leaning over as the wing swung me around, and I went shooting back along the beach above the edge of the road. I was above tree height now.

I flew over the party guests standing out in front of Cat's

place. A kid pointed to the sky, then another and another. As I whooshed past, there were about a hundred people on the stairs, on the road, and on the beach, all craning their necks into the sky. It was a hell of a moment. I wondered if Speed was down there and I wished for a second that we were filming this on something better than Paul's phone. But then I kind of realized that I didn't care. I was flying. I'd imagined this a thousand times and I wanted to stay up there forever. It was like in my dream. Nothing else mattered. It was just me and the sky.

In an upstairs window of Cat's place I could see a figure. A silhouette with the warm light of a lamp behind her. I could imagine a thousand pouting models all looking down on her and Cat looking out at me sweeping through the late afternoon sky. I imagined her smiling. I knew she wouldn't be but that's how I wanted to see her.

As I came to the northern end of the beach again, I heard my dad and Paul whooping like madmen below.

"You're flying!" Paul screamed.

"I know!" I yelled back.

I turned again and started to wonder when I might land this thing. I'd lost quite a bit of altitude. I had planned on landing at the bottom of the dune at the northern end, but I hadn't factored in Egg and the dudes waiting for me. The last thing I wanted was to hit sand and get beaten up. I started to panic a little and, in that second, everything my dad had taught me about landing was wiped from my hard drive.

But I did have to get down. Maybe I could land on McMasters and hope that the spectacle of me getting the trike in the air was enough to stun Egg temporarily.

"Bring her down gently," my dad called. "Remember what I told you!"

But I couldn't. I couldn't remember a thing. I wanted to stay up there all night, till everyone went home. I looked out over the ocean and I could see a yacht moored out there. Maybe I could land on the deck? Blowing Rock jutted out of the bay a few hundred yards offshore, but that was no place to land. There was a reason why runways weren't built out of jagged clumps of rocks surrounded by shark-infested ocean.

My mind was racing through all the options as I slowly dropped. I was only twenty yards above the beach now and soaring along the waterline.

Then it finally occurred to me that, with my dad and Paul and everyone else around, there was no way Egg would do anything to me. I decided that all I had to do was focus on landing without killing myself and the rest would take care of itself . . . hopefully.

I turned around and started heading back toward the crowd again. I adjusted the wing and began dropping steadily. Halfway through the turn, though, the onshore breeze started pushing me farther up the beach toward Cat's place. The soft sand was only about fifteen yards below me and, if I landed on that, things could get ugly. My wheels would bog down and it'd be a repeat of this morning—but at twice the speed. What I needed, desperately, was hard sand.

I tried turning again and then realized I was heading for the trees. The ground rushed by. I don't know what speed I was doing but I knew it was quick. I remember coming in toward the pines on the beachfront, branches soaring toward me and knowing, for sure, that it was all going to end in pain. I braced for the crash and tried to steer the trike clear of the trunks of the trees ahead. I was about five yards off the ground. The wing hit branches. I kept flying forward. Then I swung up into a tree. And swung back again. I was hanging by my wing. I waited for the trike to slam into the ground. But, instead, I swung forward again. Then back. And forward again.

The crowd had surged toward the tree and people were standing below, dozens of phones filming me hanging there, a whole bunch of cheering, and voices saying, "Are you okay?" and "That was awesome," and "Let's get him down."

It wasn't quite the landing I had planned but it was good to be alive.

⊰ The Real World ⊱

I woke and I didn't know what time it was. My bedroom was hot and my head felt heavy. The sun was high in the sky. There were voices and people doing things outside. I crawled to the end of my bed and looked out the window. Backpackers playing volleyball and painting masks. A girl sitting against a tree, watching everybody and sketching in a notebook. Mr. Kim serving coffee to an Indian woman at the café. The bus was silent.

I stepped out of bed, aching, and it took me a second to find my balance. I looked at my face in a little mirror. I had crusty stuff everywhere. I gave my face a rub. I wandered downstairs. Stumbled, really.

The clock on the wall over the stove said one o'clock. For a second I wondered if that was in the morning or afternoon but the sun kind of gave it away. I felt weird.

There was a message on the kitchen bench. I read it, threw on some clothes, and headed out.

A Meeting with Speed Cohen

Seagulls fought over french fries. One fat gull chased others with an evil squawk, daring them to try to steal his fries. Kids kicked water at each other. Frisbees crowded the sky. A dog panted nearby, desperate for a drink. I shoved his water bowl toward him with my foot.

It was just after two and I was sitting on the surf club balcony wearing some new clothes that Ma had left out for me. Ironed and everything. I didn't even know we had an iron. They weren't new-new, but thrift shop–new. Only one previous owner, I figured.

"Mac Daddy!" said a voice.

I turned, stood, and shook hands with Speed.

"Hey," I said.

"You want a drink?" he asked.

"Yeah, just water maybe."

"How do you feel?" he said.

"Weird."

"Yeah, well, don't worry about it. That'll pass."

Cat's vlog the previous night was shot in her room, the wall of pouting models behind her as she made her case for why she should win: "Please, please, please. I want this more than anything else in the world. I will beg you for this. The past week has made me feel like the center of the universe. I was made for doing this. I am truly destined to be somebody. This is my life," and on and on it went.

Paul and I had submitted the sketchy vid he'd shot on his phone. It was pretty bad but then we had a whole bunch of comments on our page from people who'd been at the party. They included links to videos shot on their own phones of me in the sky. There were about eighteen videos. Most of them were kind of dark but some of them were good, with me sweeping over the party, lit by the streetlights below and the orangey-gray sunset behind. If you watched a bunch of these thirty-second or one-minute clips, you got a pretty good sense of this amazing homemade flying machine cruising the night sky.

On Cat's page there were links to vids of the hailstorm—the band getting hit by massive white stones while they dragged their gear inside. There was some pretty cool footage. But it wasn't enough.

"How d'you think Cat's going to feel?" Speed asked me.

I shrugged my shoulders and had a flash of her sitting there, watching from the window. I kind of felt sorry for her. She didn't mean to be who she was.

"You ever been to New York before?" he asked.

I smiled and shook my head. "Never been anywhere," I said. "Never been on a plane."

Speed laughed.

"Where's Paul?" he said.

I shrugged again.

"Well, I want to talk to him, too," he said.

"I thought you—"

"I was wrong," he said. "Subscribers love him. He's an odd guy but he's got something, y'know. He's got a weird kind of charisma."

I stuck my fingers in my mouth and gave a whistle.

"Paul!" I said.

Paul came around the corner from his hidden table inside the surf club. I'd dropped by his place on the way. I needed him.

"Me?"

Speed laughed. "Yeah, you," he said. "Take a seat. You're going to New York."

Paul flashed his crazy teeth and pumped Speed's hand. I couldn't believe Paul'd touched him. Speed had to be thirty-five at least. And Paul actually made eye contact.

"Do you know who's gonna chaperone you?" he asked.

"Um, yeah. I think so," I said. I whistled again. "Dad!"

My dad came out from where Paul had been. We'd taken a ride up the hill and I'd convinced my dad to come meet Speed. And maybe even come to New York with me. With us.

211

Maybe. I was still working on him. He wore a tie-dyed T-shirt and some jeans cut off at the knees, with bare feet and a shoulder bag. His hair was mad but he'd shaved off his beard that morning. His face was all tanned, apart from where his beard had been. He cut a pretty wacky picture.

"Speed, this is my dad," I said. Speed shook my dad's hand.

"I know. I'd like to see your lightning farm sometime," he said. "Genius, mate."

My dad just sort of grunted. He didn't take that well to flattery.

So we all sat there, talking to Speed Cohen about cool-hunting and New York and Cat DeVrees and that whole insane week and what the future might be like.

"Does this mean we don't have to work at Taste Sensation anymore?" Paul asked.

"What's Taste Sensation?" said Speed.

"Don't ask," I warned him.

"Well, you're on the payroll now. I don't think you'll have time for another job."

"You seriously have no idea how much that means," I said to Speed.

We watched kids flying kites and gulls hovering in the wind and a little girl running down the sand dune holding a beach umbrella, desperately trying to take to the sky. And I told them all for the fifteenth time what flying had been like. And landing in a tree.

At one stage Speed was talking to my dad, and I looked over at Paul and he slid me some skin. I'll never forget the look on his face.

"We're going to New York City," he said.

"And we can fly."

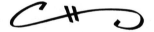

Hunt cool. Win stuff. Visit macslater.com.

Sign up for the newsletter, enter the competition, find out more about the author, and watch the trailer now!

Read on for a sneak peek from *Mac Slater: I Love NY*

Paul and I bolted the last fifty yards up Thirty-second Street toward the box office, dodging through the crowd. Dad lumbered along behind.

An Imaginator banner hung from the side of Madison Square Garden, next to a digital New York Knicks sign. The banner read,

IMAGINATOR FESTIVAL OF INVENTIONS AND CREATIVITY

MARCH 13–15

Today was March 14.

I joined Paul at the back of the short line.

"I can't believe we're actually here."

"Check that out," Paul said.

There was a girl sitting on the ground nearby, back against the wall. She was short, with dark hair and eyes. She looked like her parents must've been from someplace interesting.

"Yeah, she's pretty cute," I said.

"No, look what she's doing," Paul said, annoyed.

She was typing into a black glove on her left hand, then she put the hand up to her ear and started talking to someone.

"What is that, like, a glove phone?" I asked as we shuffled forward in line.

"Maybe you can get them here."

"Check out the skates," I said.

On her feet, she had these giant wheels. Or they were more like bowling balls set into the bottom of a pair of boots. Like one-wheel roller skates. Roller balls, maybe.

"How do you balance on those things?" Paul asked. We'd been working on a two-wheel skateboard for a couple of years, and the balance thing was a killer.

"I could film her on your phone. Why don't you go ask her for a demo?" I said.

Paul just looked at me, rolling his eyes—his *Don't be an idiot* look. We both knew by now that Paul wasn't the kind of guy who just went up and talked to humans. Especially girls.

She finished her call.

"I'm gonna go ask her," I said. "Those skates are hot."

"Next!" said a voice.

A chubby, gray-faced woman was ready to serve us. Imagine that someone Photoshopped the head of a bulldog onto the body of a rhinoceros and locked it in a ticket booth. That was her.

I took a last look at Rollergirl, hoping she wouldn't take off.

"Um, yeah, two tickets, thanks."

The bulldog stared at me. "Really?" she asked. "You two want tickets?"

I looked at Paul, then at what we were wearing. Paul looked a little uncool in his "missing link" T-shirt with the Neanderthal dude on it but surely he could still go in. "Yeah. Two tix please," I said.

"Okay. Seven-fifty each for a two-day pass. Show finishes tomorrow," she grunted.

I rustled around in my pocket for the cash Dad had given me. I tossed a ten and a five onto the counter. The woman stared at the bills.

"It's seven hundred and fifty dollars," she said.

"Are you kidding?" I said. "We don't want to buy the festival."

"Imaginator is not a public exhibition. It's a major industry conference and festival for international delegates. Now step aside please, sir."

Paul began moving away but I stood there. I didn't want to have to pull this card, but . . . "We're from Coolhunters," I said.

"The website." She gave me that same bitter, bulldog stare. If she was a real dog I'd have started backing up real slow.

"Good for you," she said. "Now step aside."

I wanted to chuck her a doggy treat and say, "Chew on this." But I didn't. I moved off.

"Why didn't you know this?" Paul asked.

"Me?"

"Yeah, you. You're the one who lured me here for this," he said.

"As if. What, you don't have the Web at home?" I said. "You couldn't have looked at the site?"

"You were, like, in charge. You kept on talking about it. I figured you might have looked at the prices!" he said.

If we were at home in our workshop I'd have wrestled him to the ground and sat on him, but there was a security dude nearby who looked ready to deport us.

"That ticket lady's a treat, isn't she?" It was Rollergirl. Standing on her skates now, gently rolling back and forth.

"Yeah," I said. "I mean, not really. Can't you get in either?"

"Nope. I'm Melody," she said.

"Hey. Good to meet you."

"You have a name?"

"Mac. Sorry. And Paul."

Paul's eyes were fixed on her glove. Mine drifted to her skates.

"I heard your accents," she said. "Where are you guys from?"

I liked the way she said "you guys."

"Kings Bay. It's halfway around the world from here," I said.

"Get outta here. I've heard of Kings Bay. It's like the coolest surfing town in the world."

"Really?" I said.

"Absolutely right," she said, the conversation kind of dying. "Bummer about the fest. I even tried flirting with the security guy but he's unbreakable."

"There's gotta be some way in," I said. "We came thousands of miles for this."

"Yeah, well, *bonne chance*," she said, and started rolling away.

"Hey, can I have a look at your glove . . . thing?" Paul said.

She turned back.

"Um, sure," she said, not looking so certain.

"What does it do?" Paul asked.

"Well, it's a kind of laptop. I call it a handtop. And it's a phone and Internet device. It's pretty much whatever you want it to be."

"Where did you get it?" I asked.

"Well, I kind of made it myself."

Paul and I looked up at her. "No way," Paul said.

"Yeah way."

"We're inventors too," I said. "Are you gonna sell these or . . ."

She started rolling backward again. "Not really. Look, I gotta go. Nice to meet you guys." She gave us a wave and skated off.

"Can you tell me about your skates?" I called.

"I'm late," she said above the noise of traffic and crowd. People were crisscrossing between us now. But I couldn't let her go. She was a coolhunter's dream.

"Is there someplace we can catch up? Or can we get your digits?"

She kept on rolling backward. Then she called out something like: "FenderBender167646."

"What?" I yelled.

But she was gone, skating off down Seventh Avenue. It wasn't like regular skating. She just kept her feet together, leaned forward, and the balls drove her forward.

"What the hell is FenderBender167646?" I asked Paul.

"Not 'FenderBender.' FriendBender. And she said, '17464.'"

"Yeah, well, what's that?" I said, unzipping my bag to grab a pen.

"I d'know. Maybe it's a street," he said.

"Yeah, FriendBender Street. Right," I said, writing *Friendbender 17464* on my hand.

"You're not falling in love again?" Paul asked.

"Shut up," I said. He always accused me of falling in love with any girl we met. I think it was because he was always hot on the chicks but he didn't have the guts to do anything about it.

"She's gone, anyway. Let's go check e-mail. See if Speed and Tony have e'd us."

"Yeah, right," Paul said. "They ditched us at the airport and won't even answer their phones. Like we'll ever hear from those idiots again."

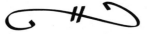

Mac and Paul are officially lost in New York. And they don't know it yet but they've stumbled across a girl who will lead them to the coolest thing in the city. Maybe even the world. But they're not allowed to tell a soul. . . .

Coming in 2011

About the Author

Tristan Bancks is a writer and filmmaker. He has a background as an actor and television host in Australia and the United Kingdom. His short films have won a number of awards and have screened widely in festivals and on TV. He loves to discover new places, hang out with his family, play sports, get lost inside a good story, and eat spicy food. His drive is to tell inspiring fast-moving stories for young people. More at tristanbancks.com.